# OUTBOUND SPIRITS

*A Novel*

## *Debra M Brose*

ISBN: 1502768755
ISBN 13: 9781502768759
Library of Congress Control Number: 2014918219
CreateSpace Independent Publishing Platform
North Charleston, South Carolina

*This story is dedicated to my parents, Shirley and William Brose.*
*I also want to acknowledge all who have inspired me and contributed to the creative process.*

# PROLOGUE

The nuns spoke French—at least to each other. If a stranger appeared, they reverted to English.

"Yes?" The sister at the door faced the couple with the baby. A month of cruel temperatures and winds led her to motion them inside with no more than the casual query. A delicate wash of icy snow swirled, settled, and wet the warm entrance of the convent.

The young woman averted her eyes from the nun's habit, holding the baby closer. Sister Genevieve, assuming there was an infant under the wraps, spoke evenly.

"How can I help you? Are you traveling?" She looked between the two. The female looked expressionless yet not without intelligence.

"Can you take them? Both of them?" His voice was probing and emotional. He removed his hood and scarf and then, tenderly and carefully, the woman's. Then he continued. "I have to go away, overseas. I can't explain, but she hasn't been right since the baby. She doesn't say a word—it may have been too much for her. And neither of us have family around here. I'll be back in six months or so."

The other nun tried to gather as much information as she could, there in the foyer, by observing the couple closely. He looked much healthier than she. Her face was gaunt, and her body was thin; he was muscular and brisk. Matching gold wedding bands and decent clothing. The woman pressed herself into his neck and sobbed with no words. The infant was stirring now. The man encouraged the woman to settle herself, and all attention was turned toward the infant.

"Sir, we need you to come in and sit down and provide us with more detailed information. We should see to the baby first, away from the cold air, and then sort this out," Sister Therese stated practically. Sister Genevieve was attempting to help calm the mother and convince her to follow them to a sitting room situated next to the entrance.

The enormous fireplace was strangely ornate within its simple surroundings. Exotic carved images elegantly gleamed from the mantle to the ceiling: elephants, lush leafy vines, and waterfalls, misplaced among modest furnishings. Straight and sturdy uncomfortable chairs had been placed simply for seating and nothing else. No decor, other than the fireplace, appealed to the beholder.

The young woman nursed the baby, while still not speaking. She had composed herself, yet she could hardly take her eyes off her husband, as if terrified he would abandon her.

Sister Genevieve, confident the mother and child were somewhat settled, asked, "Now tell us, what is your family's situation? How did you end up at our door?" Her voice was steady but firmer than previously.

"She needs some help. I can't make out why she won't speak. She seems OK with the baby, but I can't be with her all the time." He was standing and pacing now. The nuns waited patiently for further details.

"Your names, sir? Where do you live? And did you say something about going abroad?" Sister Genevieve felt they were all getting closer to understanding the visitor's plight. If they could get the girl to speak and open up, perhaps the story would unfold.

With no warning the young woman collapsed in her chair, slumping to the floor, the infant sliding from her arms down before her, only to be snatched by the quick reaction of Sister Therese, who didn't even manage a gasp.

The nuns moved her onto her back and placed her coat over her to keep her covered on the floor. "Her breath is shallow but steady. We need to get a doctor." Sister Genevieve's voice trailed off as she looked to instruct the baby's father. The convent sitting room was noticeably chilled and suddenly silent: the front door, wide open; the anxious man, vanished.

# CHAPTER 1
# THE BLACKSMITH

*Renfrew County, Ontario, Canada—1910*

"Steady..." Josef leaned over yet again to examine his work in the glow of the coal fire and what remained of the daylight. He had felt distracted and uneasy all day, but a man couldn't let his mood keep him from making a living.

Assessing his craft unlike an ordinary person, his eyes strained to measure the detail of the horseshoe. "There," he proclaimed. The horse had lowered its foot in a natural way, settled it on the ground, and appeared comfortable.

After leading the animal out of the shelter of the stable and carefully observing its gait, he glanced around but noticed nothing unusual—nothing approaching on the quiet road lined with firs and cedars. He returned his attention to the matter at hand; when he felt uncertain, it was always best to be working.

Vaguely aware of her presence, Josef was nonetheless startled when Elise interrupted his attempt at shaking off his unsettledness. "That horse never has been here before, has it?" she said. "Is that why you're concentrating so hard?"

Unable to explain, he conceded. "Yes, it belongs to someone important. Go in the house and help your mother and sister. I'll be along shortly."

Elise and Marie had been born in his and Giselle's home. He could hear the mix of lighthearted conversation and slightly frustrated encouragement from Giselle coming from the direction of the kitchen window.

Josef listened with amusement for a minute and then surveyed his property intensely while maintaining a relaxed, still stance. He was looking at what he observed every spring. Strong signs of the earth's emergence into the fertile season were evident. Pungent foliage decay had been revealed after the melt, and newly warmed cedar bows uniquely scented the valley.

The smell of rich life-giving soil stirred *some* people deeply, he realized: those who worked it, and who were continually frantic about its condition as well as the weather—the damn weather. How much rain would fall? Would there be warmth, and was it too late or too early? Would the heat of the sun be a glorious offering or the harbinger of a slow death? The timing of the weather conditions and how they affected the crops were all they could think about. *All that hoping and praying to God that the battle will go their way*, Josef thought.

It was all-consuming for them, but he came from a different place—his heart, which was no different from his father's. Just like his father had been, Josef was devoted to his craft, unyielding and obsessed with mastering the metal.

His shop stood on the low road, close to the river that snaked its way through the valley and the village. Fifty years prior Loren hadn't existed, except as a small camp stop for timber and steamboat crews. It was on the third chute of the Helle River and boasted several businesses, including a sawmill and a gristmill.

The white pines were thinning out, and the pristine river floated less and less of the superior wood, sold mostly for shipbuilding. Josef's father had insisted that "well-traveled buyers will pay dearly for it."

But a fact of life is that things evolve, and when the demand had ebbed, the village dwellers had shifted, adapted, and most of them, through hard work, had thrived.

Josef's father had been one of them. The shop was his then, as was the house with walls now three feet thick. The home, built years prior, was first assembled from logs, a clumsy two-room construction performed by a tired settler and an equally exhausted wife. Later a second layer of stacked shale was added, along with a few extra rooms. When Josef was a boy, the house was redone again, with fir planks and plaster. He couldn't remember the details, but a layer of brick was added a few years later, and now there stood a beautiful redbrick house, complete with a separate parlor, kitchen, and dining room. The Reicher home, blacksmith shop, and stable all made for a solid, respectable property.

It was amazing how Giselle had barely aged in their thirteen years of marriage. They hadn't been too young for marriage: he, twenty-five, and Giselle, twenty. They had held to their dream for a family and home and never strayed from it.

Josef's father wouldn't have wanted him to think about his mood. *Just keep working, and things will sort themselves out*, he thought. Giselle had often remarked how much he was like his father. He had passed not long after they were married. Josef's above-average height and pale-blond hair were his father's, as well as

Elise's. Marie had her mother's dark coloring, excluding the blue eyes. Josef had passed those down.

He returned to the present and focused on the horseshoe, inwardly cursing while trying to remember whether his wedding anniversary was tomorrow or the next day.

His passion for his craft often led him to another place in his mind; he was so dedicated to perfection. He had profited in life, which was solidly evidenced in his accounts but mostly in his soul.

Josef had labored hard for his assets and provided a comfortable life for his family. Yet, always, in the back of his mind, he wondered whether his focus was a subconscious distraction to avoid ultimately facing not being able to pass down his business, as had been done for several generations, to a son.

That, he surmised, would unfold as the universe intended, as he surely had done his part. He had successfully let go of that worry for several years—and would for many more if he chose to—but for some reason, his long-passed-away father and the fate of his business were on his mind today.

Dismissing the thoughts with stern intention, he smiled, thinking of his daughters, and proud of himself for now remembering for certain that the day in question was tomorrow. It would be amusing, though, if he let on to the girls that he had forgotten and even more amusing if their mother believed it for a moment—but Giselle would never suspect him of having a serious memory lapse. His heart felt somewhat lighter again.

A harsh rumbling arose in an inhospitable crescendo from the road, its source too far away to be visible yet. That sound, once strange and frightening to humans and animals, was now only briefly startling to those who heard it. It was becoming less of an oddity. Even infrequently traveled roads were now groomed for the new species. Everyone wanted to make the world a more connected and accessible place.

Josef soon realized it was an automobile. There weren't many around, and this one was struggling with the spring conditions of the usually horse-driven road. He chose not to acknowledge it visually, but the noise commanded his attention, and he couldn't help wonder about certain things. Had his father seen the madness coming? Metal and steel, bent and fabricated in ways unimaginable. Assembly lines and steelworkers—as they were now called—helped machines make machines. And he heard more and more talk of great things to come. Some even predicted a life that might no longer revolve around horses and stables, a world with independent, mechanical travel only—no livestock unless it was for work. Where would all this eventually leave the blacksmiths and farriers?

Josef, feeling philosophical yet uneasy, anticipated a possible late-evening opportunity to speculate about these mysteries of life with his comrades, especially Will Frank, a man committed to another precarious vocation: harness making.

He, Will, and Maxwell Loren (the village mayor) often kept company to amuse, inspire, and encourage one another. Although they were very different, these three souls complemented one another, with Josef the hardest working and only family man of the three; Will, ever hopeful and creatively competitive with his leather business; and Maxwell, by far, the wealthiest and most secretive. Maxwell was secretive yet not withdrawn—prone to bouts of ranting and ill-tempered carrying on. Josef and Will were often left wondering if the mayor's tales of business acquaintances abroad were fabricated or real.

"I call this beloved province my home but am from another continent and spent my childhood on a third; there is always a place for me in other parts of the world. This little valley appealed to my father for whatever reason—I will be satisfied to continue on in this dalliance of a business," Loren would proclaim as the whiskey saturated his bloodstream.

Presumably he had access to significant family wealth, as the gristmill, while flourishing, couldn't support the kind of lifestyle he led. He returned to the United Kingdom for several months out of the year—though he remained reluctant to share details with his friends about his travels, other than how he suffered from wanderlust.

"Did your father mill grain in India or Chestershire?" Josef had probed, knowing the answer but wondering if perhaps he would elaborate as he drank more.

"He did, and he bought and sold fine furniture, art, and tea, at first for his collections, and then he molded a healthy business between the two countries—of great benefit to both. It changed—slowed down with all the damn regulations and laws. There are other things I could supply..." The mayor's voice had trailed, and his focus shifted inward. He wondered if he'd sufficiently piqued their interest.

That night Josef didn't feel like biting the bait and shifted the topic. "The automobiles—I feel the pressure. Giselle suggests farming, but it's not for me. Can I make that big of a shift and still feel the same about my work as I do now? Not likely."

"Feel the same about your work?" Loren needed clarification. "Are you a painter, an artist? No—you are making an honest living. You are good at the metalworking; you will be good at something else."

"Not if I don't see the sense in it or have the family trait—I disagree. Do you see a man's work as either innate artistic talent or strictly bank-account business? Nothing in between? I believe they cross over." Josef was in a place where he was comfortable—defending his craft and his love of it.

Will sensed a need to form some type of bland conclusion, or this particular debate would go on for hours. "We can't ignore the need to make a living. All three of us own a business. What emotional level we embrace it at is an individual choice—I say the line is not very definitive at all." If Maxwell had a few more under his belt, the harness shop would be subject to witty criticism—and the reality of it made Will cringe.

"Nope. Not interested in farming at all, really." Josef wasn't going to show even a slight sign of conceding. There was a beauty in that for him: staying true to his calling, his family, and beliefs. How could a man live any other way? Giselle would come around and understand. She was panicking and thinking only of the children, naturally.

# CHAPTER 2
# THE HARNESS MAKER

Will Frank stood outside his business, assessing the newly glossed pressed board. "Gloss paint," they'd told him at the general store. "It weathers better. More eye-catching." He likely would have many boastful conversations about the new storefront. FRANK'S LEATHER GOODS appeared in gold-outlined scarlet letters on a pristine white background.

A few years prior, the fantasy of the automobile had seemed unimaginable to Will, but now the pace of production and its accessibility had pushed the harness maker into the extensive, but nonetheless awkward, expansion of leather provisions for paying customers. A new modern sign gave the impression of a thriving business, and his recent relocation to the center of town offered proof that he was moving ahead with the times.

But Will knew it was no more than a false front. Horsepower was, in fact, no longer horsepower, and that knowledge had set a cold, stony feeling in him.

He had carried on his father's work. Still alive and living under Will's roof, his elderly father was frail and soft spoken. Barely audible, he sometimes probed his son in the hopes that he would find, hidden in some magical conversation, his youth, bright and sparkling and better than it really had been.

"Will, did you fit some fine animals today?" he'd ask. "Did they need some custom-made work? Did your customers pay a decent price?"

Will wondered whether his father loved horses more than he had loved his deceased wife. Occasionally the old man wandered through the shop, but the improvements and changes went unacknowledged. He railed against the advent of the automobile and was convinced they would serve only greedy folks; good, God-fearing people would go to church on foot or on a horse.

Will saw his father withdrawing from the present before his eyes, sadness being the only detectable emotion. *Was it like that for everyone as they got old?* he wondered.

"Dad, we should visit the cemetery soon. It's been a few months." Would this tidbit of reality get through?

"How long has she been gone, again? I can't remember right now."

"Four years." Will didn't know what to make of this.

"I can't quite remember how it all happened. Can you tell me?" The old man appeared calm and was making a clearly stated request.

"She just slipped away, Dad, over several years, all quiet-like." Will kept his eyes on his father's face.

"Where did she slip to?"

"She was admitted to an institution in Ottawa for mental-health issues. Remember?"

Will's mother had grown more distant and silent since his teen years, until she had refused to speak altogether and stopped taking care of herself, much less Will and his father. Until now his father hadn't mentioned her since the day she had died. Her death coincidentally and precisely marked the day he had become weak and sickly and stopped working. He waited in the evenings to hear about the day's events from his son but showed little interest in venturing out to the business area of the property. Will wasn't sure he wanted him speaking to customers anyway.

He reflected on his last visit with Josef and Maxwell, his primary sources of socializing. One or both of them had prodded him lately about being alone too much and especially chided him for spending most evenings with his father.

"Good God, man," the mayor had chided, after downing his second shot before the other two were done pouring their first, "you'll forget how to speak English if the only company you keep is your father's."

He wondered whether they had any inkling about his last trip to the bakery and his conversation with Laura.

"Do you get up really early to bake everything?" he ventured to ask nearly every time he entered the establishment.

Her reply was standard but enthusiastic. "I do! Every day I bake all of it fresh."

Her blushing confused him. Was she one of those females who blushed during most conversations? She seemed receptive to his presence, but was she being polite to a somewhat older suitor? Or was she self-conscious about their age difference and embarrassed, hoping he'd never return?

He guessed she was barely twenty but very mature and responsible. He had been told by many he was baby-faced and looked young for being in his midthirties—this should work in his favor. Surely Laura could respect an established bachelor with his own business.

Will knew it was up to him to take the conversation to the next level. He had to speak on a new topic, and it had to be more personal and possibly allude to the possibility of Laura accompanying him somewhere outside of her workplace.

On this particular occasion—a most stunning spring day—his courage matched the momentum of the season. Will placed his hands on the counter and leaned forward to face Laura directly, his vulnerability and trust corralled between them like a petrified baby farm animal. She looked startled and waited for him to speak. He came out with it.

"Do you think it would be possible for us to see each other somewhere other than here?" He couldn't believe he had put it in those terms. No matter— instantly he saw her reaction. Her smile was enormous, and he was certain his relief filled the bakery with an audible presence. The sound, however, was actually the greeting of a young man who had stepped through the door behind Will and was the intended recipient of Laura's smile.

"Excuse me…" The new face stepped in front of Will, as if he weren't there, and engaged Laura in some exuberant, youthful conversation.

Will, taking his fresh rolls as fast as he could and praying she hadn't heard him, bolted. Taking deep gulps of the fresh spring air, he hoped to steady himself before returning to his shop.

He hadn't experienced much female company other than Laura's, and Josef and Maxwell could never know what had happened.

Before this last encounter, Will could nicely imagine getting together with her somehow, but what would his father do if, on one or two evenings a week, he didn't dote on him? He didn't know how to broach that topic and decided to let it be for now. Bachelorhood wasn't all that bad. If he were honest with himself, he would have to admit he might be waiting for his father to pass on before he would court a woman. Plus the thought of more rejection left him jittery.

He had best be thinking of work and work only. He had put all that effort into the new storefront after all and even had made trips to other towns and villages to see what the competition looked like. *Very entrepreneurial*, he thought.

Will had something important to work on; these days it seemed trendy to have a slogan sign in one's business window. The leather goods were in a small store, while the harness-fitting area was outdoors, under a shelter. Would a slogan stop the panic he felt?

Although he attempted to keep his angst well hidden, he was sure people were starting to notice it, which made him even more anxious.

Josef's company, however, was relaxing, and Will always looked forward to their conversations, especially regarding what to make of progress and the world around them. Will appreciated how perceptive and intuitive Josef was; he seemed to have an almost supernatural perception as to how things unfolded in his life, predicting things more accurately than most. Josef put it down to his upbringing and "learning the hard way when not using mankind's gift: the unique ability to reason"—one of his favorite expressions.

Sometimes their conversations took place in the comfort of one of their homes, but mostly they happened at one of their businesses at dusk, accompanied by a few shots of whiskey, their mutual respect and encouragement keeping their cold fears about life at bay. Maxwell usually joined them, even inviting them to his elegant home on the west side of the Helle, perched on a bluff with a view that made the town his not only by namesake, but also due to the home's position on the outer end of the high road.

Will experienced the wave of modernization with trepidation and fascination simultaneously. It was forcing him to leave the old-school beliefs about running the family business. Whether or not he was comfortable with it wasn't relevant. He wondered why Maxwell hadn't, with all his wealth, shown more interest in investing in updating the exterior of the gristmill. The mayor invested in fine horses and even an automobile, and his home was spectacular. The blacksmith and the mayor were convinced Will didn't share a passion for his business the way they did. A little sprucing up of the storefront was interesting for a bit, but something else seemed to be on Will's mind. They couldn't quite put a finger on it.

Already Will had heard talk of the town of replacing the gas lamps with electrically powered streetlamps. The possible presence of wires over the streets, like snakes in trees, didn't concern him; he liked the finer things in life and welcomed progress and modernization in theory, but the reality is that he worried it would jeopardize his livlihood.

Industry in Loren thrived, with no threat posed in these progressive times to lumber or grain. Farmers hauled cans of cream and milk to the local dairy, which was newly sophisticated, with a front-end sales area to display and sell products.

The village had two bakeries, one at either end of Main Street. One offered painstakingly created dainties, soft rolls, and cakes—with something unexpected and unique provided daily—presented as sweet art. Will preferred that bakery because of Laura. The other sold thickly crusted hearty breads and was conveniently attached to a grocery and open longer hours.

There was no shortage of scenery in the village, as local business owners competitively strived to adorn their shops and doorways. The two churches, built in sparkling-white limestone, welcomed and heartened all who attended. The seeds of prosperity and culture had been planted and had produced perennial flora, each year taking firmer root.

Oblivious to the people and sounds, the Helle, steady and wide, ran through the middle of town under an arched bridge. The river was the soul of the surrounding land and its dwellers. They lived mostly unaware of its hypnotic flow, which was constant and especially powerful in the spring. The river, a time-less constant, rushing but never changing, seemed virtually unaffected by the progress that was taking place all around it.

The harness maker didn't delve too deeply into philosophy, but he understood what his two friends embraced and had pressed into their core beings. Maxwell appreciated the river only in the black of night, from afar, when it amused him and appeared like a jewel. Josef wanted his craft to be the river but didn't realize it was.

The river, after all, eventually made its way out of familiar territory to unknown landscapes full of treachery, invisible to the here and now.

# CHAPTER 3
# THE MAYOR

Maxwell Loren drew back the wine-colored velvet drapes and gazed out his polished parlor window at the sparkling river and village. It was a warm spring evening, perfect for relaxation and reflection. He stood quietly and played out a remembered confrontation—a scene of uncivilized perfection—over and over in his mind. Each time he mused over it, he marveled at the purity of the crude emotions, the amazing simplicity of human behavior, on his part and that of the farmer.

He searched for his favorite pipe, a purchase made by his father while visiting India when Maxwell was a child. After he retrieved it, he waited for his tea to be served on the brass trolley, one of many treasured wares his family had brought from England.

His father had loved India and seen to it that Maxwell had spent his childhood there. He had been raised by servants on a plantation—playing with their children, running freely in joyous oblivion. Something of a serious nature, however, always temporarily brought them around to reality and the harshness of where they lived, despite appearances: snakebites, lost children, tropical diseases, and the terse anger of the people whose country had been invaded by his kind.

A chill gripped him for a moment—for a moment only, as he had learned how to steady himself with this particularly frightening memory, how to not let it run away with his emotions. There was confusing shouting everywhere, a wailing father of his playmate shaking him like a dusty mat, demanding to know what happened to his son. They had been at the edge of a shallow river, throwing rocks, their backs to the trees along the shore, playing the game they always played, throwing small rocks toward the reeds, laughing and shouting at each other—imagining all the things six-year-old boys' minds let them. The other boy was silenced so quickly it was impossible to imagine anything bad had happened. That part was quick—the almost soft thudding sound of contact and the deep

21

exhalation of the enormous cat's breath as it struck. Had it flown from the sky? Maxwell had no idea—and the worst part was recalling a deep rumbling purr emanating from the muscular striped body. He could hear nothing else as it flew off with his playmate, in one or two bounds back into the trees, gone forever. There were no loud sounds, no screaming, no blood, and no trace of what happened. Had he been looking away or ducking under the water, he wouldn't even have known what happened to the boy.

The locals were out of control. They wanted to know why the Indian boy had been taken while the clearly imperfect English boy with the bad foot hadn't. Maxwell's mother didn't need any more reason to return to England. She insisted the three of them return—Maxwell's father couldn't persuade her that the effects of the tragedy would pass if she could just be patient.

He was too young to fully understand her frustration—the most notable realization for him being the simplicity and grace of the cat. It was motivated by survival instincts, hungry and opportunistic—nothing more complicated than that.

The pipe was the only object that had survived, a reminder of that time in Maxwell's father's life. Not even the exotic Indian artwork his father cherished remained. His mother had seen to that. She hated their trips to India and had disposed of the artifacts and memories as quickly as his father's mind had slipped in his last few years.

Maxwell admired his mother's traits, however—especially her style and decor, which were still alive and well in the house—and he took naturally to his surroundings. Pastoral scenes were intermittent on the walls, with framed interludes of English country gardens on the brocade wallpaper, left to him as part of a lifestyle she had reassured herself he would carry on with. He had also inherited her slight stature and dark coloring—and stoic British demeanor until even gingerly provoked.

Maxwell abandoned the window and stretched out on the cognac-colored leather sofa. The room was arranged in a very particular manner, especially the artwork. His gaze could rest, while he reposed, on the Friedrich that brooded on the opposite wall. It contrasted with the lighthearted beauty of the other works. He pondered the dark branches, which were devoid of greenery, against the cold background. Jagged spears pierced the cemetery foreground. Each element was nothing special on its own, but together they formed a formidable image that created the eeriest of atmospheres.

The painting never failed to captivate him. Who occupied the graves? What would it be like to be part of that setting, all alone in the dark shadows and frosty air, with God knows who or what?

Cold, gray solitude in death—there was no choice in that, he knew. But in life? That was another matter altogether. People could get what they wanted if they stayed on course—plenty of choices and opportunities.

"Here you are, sir." The housekeeper made an entrance with the fragrant brew through the archway from the dining room. They performed this charade every evening. She served tea, and then he let it sit, untouched, while he poured several brandies.

He'd had the massive, looming house remodeled somewhat since his parents had died and had several sets of garden doors installed in the wall that faced the river. Most times in the evening, he was alone with his thoughts and therefore had made his manor as stately and agreeable as possible.

No woman had entered his life, but that was not because he couldn't provide more than any man in Renfrew County or he wasn't held in high esteem; he guessed it was his slight physical imperfection: a withered left foot that turned inward. It had been weak from birth. The curve prevented proper muscle use, and the atrophy had occurred before he was four. He learned to get around with minimal difficulty. There had been various braces as an infant—none of consequence. His mother's overprotective attitude had been tempered by his father, to some degree, but mostly the foot had not been discussed aloud. He maintained, privately, that an intelligent woman would see past that, and perhaps this county didn't in fact hold a formidable female character worthy of him.

Maxwell visualized the amusing scenario again. On a recent afternoon that beckoned him outdoors, he stepped into the street in front of the gristmill, passing his automobile, as he desired a midday ride on his favorite horse to clear his head of frustrating business issues. Inside the office, the trivialities of local folk in his employ made him want to strike them down or fantasize about it at least. How could they lead such petty lives? He seldom walked any considerable distance, as his impediment was much more obvious while he was on foot. He must not be seen disadvantaged.

He had rounded the perimeter of his mill and entered the stable at the back, where his good-tempered mare was waiting. Ignoring the slight distraction of an intense conversation coming from the back of the mill, possibly escalating to argumentative levels, he led her into the back lane and mounted. The horse had covered barely any ground, a mere ten steps, though, it became clear that her front left leg was uncomfortable.

Maxwell gently urged her forward to eliminate the possibility of a temporary cramp and went to the front street. The horse, however, still appeared tender in the hoof; this matter would require some professional attention. Providentially, the blacksmith, Josef Reicher, appeared from a building across the street.

"Hey there, Reicher! My mare seems to be a bit lame on the front left!"

"Hang on." Josef nodded and crossed to assist the mayor.

That's when the farmer appeared, Ivan Hauffe, shouting in an amalgam of English and German that Maxwell couldn't understand much of. His large frame was stiff with hostility, blue eyes snapping. He did manage to pick up on the fact that the man's ire was directed at him, regarding the price the gristmill had paid the farmer for grain.

As he wasn't a big supplier, the buyers in the back likely had worked him over a bit. After a failed attempt to ignore the outburst, Maxwell encouraged the horse to move forward, but the farmer interfered by jumping in front, startling the already-upset animal and causing it to rear. Firmly mounted after narrowly evading being toppled, the mayor laughed as the farmer stumbled and fell hard on the road.

Not about to let an opportunity slip by, Maxwell chided the immigrant for his failed attack. "What the hell are you at? Whatever it is, you're the downed man here! You're nothing more than an ignorant fool!"

"I know you hate all farm people! You want to tell me what my grain is worth and decide how I get paid to feed my family," the farmer snapped, his uncontrolled frustration in plain view. He was roaring for the sake of roaring and gesturing with his fist.

Maxwell smugly remembered how childish it had seemed. How could the bloody man not expect what had happened? Did he not own a horse? And yet he had behaved as though Maxwell had encouraged the animal to knock him down, and he, perhaps, thought the horse was out to get him too.

The farmer had taken the price of the grain personally and couldn't keep himself level to discuss the matter in a businesslike manner. Maxwell, as a perceptive businessman, felt qualified to read people and decided the farmer wasn't anywhere near being capable of displaying mature, rational behavior.

A further shouting match ensued. Neither could be heard over the other's rant. The farmer was beginning to lose his voice. Josef was assessing the best way to subdue the man.

Fully aware of being at a physical disadvantage if he dismounted, Maxwell stayed put. Josef saw his opportunity and lunged at Hauffe. He grabbed him and faced him away and toward the mayor, not so much to make him vulnerable but to ensure he didn't get spit on or bitten.

Once Josef had fully restrained the farmer from behind, the mayor gave the man a firm lecture on how he should learn the language of the country he was living in, as his speech was a disgrace.

Now that the flailing and kicking were over, Josef hoped Maxwell would carry on with his business, but he was bitterly disappointed. There were onlookers, and the stage was set for humiliating the man; the mayor couldn't resist grandstanding and gave the curious crowd a satisfying performance.

"Folks! Take note of this incoherent spectacle of a man! Should I use my whip to tame him?" Maxwell's decision to carry on and ridicule the farmer proved erroneous, as now the man appeared even more hostile.

Josef gently told the mayor it was time to drop the issue. After catching the farmer off guard with a shake to bring him to his senses, he let him go, causing him to be still for a moment before bolting back to wherever he had come from.

The blacksmith was transfixed with shock. Relief slowly seeped into his being, but the whole scene was surreal and had left him deeply concerned and bewildered. Fortunately, the dust was settling, and the small crowd had quieted.

Only the mayor vocalized his thoughts and eventually drew Josef into a conversation. "I will certainly require your services," he told him. "This horse is tender at the front left." Maxwell had recovered unusually quickly from the altercation, leaving the blacksmith wondering whether perhaps he had enjoyed it. It made Josef slightly uncomfortable to see his friend drag out the scenario, but he dismissed it quickly. He often found himself second-guessing his own intuition, and it could be aggravating at times.

Josef and Maxwell remained on the street for a half hour, trying to make sense of what had happened, and presumed it to be the manifestation of some kind of manic fit or episode of mental illness. Will approached from down the street to join them and find out what had transpired.

"It looked like your horse was out of control—did anyone get struck?" Will was looking at Maxwell, who shook his head.

"Inarguably and undoubtedly an unpredictable lunatic," Maxwell snorted.

"He attacked you?" Will now searched Josef's face for more explanation.

"He was arguing with Maxwell over the price of grain. It escalated into larger proportions for no good reason. Those types are easily worked around but best given a wide berth," Josef observed. He also observed, privately, that Maxwell seemed determined to proclaim insanity on the part of the farmer and perceived himself to be completely innocent. Josef then invited his friend to his home to, at the very least, deliver the horse for inspection. "If you want to make a social call at the same time," he added, "Giselle and I will be happy to accommodate."

"I'll accompany you there now if it's convenient," he answered. Maxwell, for a variety of reasons, always enjoyed spending time at the Reichers' home.

*Now that was a most interesting encounter,* he thought, as he relaxed on the sofa and sipped his brandy. *People can be so predictable and amusing at the same time.*

# CHAPTER 4
# THE BREW MAKER

A few miles away in the hills, life lay in stark contrast from life in Loren, with some who didn't
connect with mainstream society living in solitude.

The shack was virtually lost in the slopes of fir
and shale. It wasn't in among the bright openings of
the landscape, where massive rocks loomed and deafening torrents of spring runoff sped toward larger
bodies of water. It was hidden, where magnificence
receded into bogs and low-sinking spots, where shadows and fractured light made it difficult to pick out
a trail.

In these dense, dark landings—some of them
unexpectedly sprawling, covered in creeping wild
vines and mosslike vegetation and smelling faintly

rotten—one could hide anything, for years if necessary, undetected by the keenest tracker.

The massive, ancient oaks, pines, and tamaracks—with their roots twisting above ground, over the dead-fir-needle floor—could break bones were a human or animal to take a wrong step. Only the brightest days allowed filtered light to penetrate; soft streams of sunlight pooled and rested temporarily in spots among the hidden depths of murkiness.

Living a full day's trek away from any of the local villages or farmers' fenced land, Jon Lewis was born in the back bush and would never leave. There was no need to. This was where those who didn't fit into a tidy, well-defined category lived, with no taxes, neighbors, or complications of community. As long as he didn't bother with them—those who found him odd—existence in the woods worked well.

He was waiting in the yard outside the shack. When the men arrived, he would lead them on the last part of their journey. He hadn't done previous business with these two nor with the possible third man; he had heard that one might be from closer by, not a complete stranger.

Uncertain whether he was comfortable dealing with these three when his sons weren't around, Jon casually checked out the weapons he had hidden in various spots. The constant moisture in the summer and winter required that he regularly clean them to avoid a misfire or jam. In the last ten years, he'd had little reason to navigate toward his guns while doing business, but one could never be too careful.

Most often, by the time his visitors arrived, their prevailing sentiment was gratitude, as well as a need to rest if they weren't on horseback. Hidden out here as he was, there was no chance of an automobile making its way to him. He hadn't seen a Mountie or any other constable for a few years.

Jon laughed, remembering the last time. The young constable, eager to find glory and triumph in the backwoods, strode in and out of the shack and paced around what he believed to be Jon's property. He must have been tipped off by some do-gooder who couldn't stand the popularity of the brew. The yard, such as it was, was undefined by fences yet clearly defined to its owner. The force of his badge and honor propelled him to investigate.

He was good natured enough, Jon deduced. The long gun remained with his horse, and the service sidearm on his belt remained in its holster, while he thrashed the trees and dense growth with his billy club, tearing at anything he thought might be concealing hard evidence of distilled liquor. Clearly the local lore had gotten to him, and he was feeling informed and determined enough to take down the operation.

Jon had remained passive, managing a confused, submissive demeanor. That's mostly what the cop had been there for in the first place—to see him worried like a dog, tossed from a boat to drown, paddling like hell; to have him squirm under the reach of the law as he was hauled off to jail.

Why on earth did the constable come alone? He must have been new to the force and perhaps new to the area as well, as he didn't have a damned clue about geography. Even more ridiculous was the notion that the brew might be near Jon's home.

It likely seemed longer for the constable, but an hour or two passed before he finally gave up his search, issued a stern verbal warning, and then rode back to his post to make a report of having found nothing.

Uncomplicated business was what Jon believed in, which had evolved from when he was a young man. He kept quiet and lived a simple life. Anyone could make brew, but the challenge was in concealing large batches. Once you solved that, the rest was easy. He believed in never getting lost (know your markers in the bush) and never cheating his customers.

Every day he thanked God for the beauty of the wilderness and the natural cover, especially the caves—miles of caverns, constantly cool and quiet, safely hidden under the rock shields. These prehistoric homes now held nothing but bats, but they didn't go as far back as a person could. The bats roosted after the first or second curve in the cave, which provided natural protection. The occasional black bear or big cat wandered in but only briefly. They liked the smaller caves, not the large ones Jon used. He preferred the ones that looked like small caverns upon entry and then expanded unexpectedly behind an innocent-looking corner.

Some years brought higher water levels underground, but they subsided after spring. He never left bottles or kegs in those areas, as they could get washed away and were costly to replace; not to mention, it was difficult to keep a fire going for light and warmth amid such dampness. Production, therefore, was restricted to the warm seasons—it was too risky to make the brew in heated buildings, where it would be easy to find—and the caves made perfect storage areas for the finished products.

He had perfected the cooking process in large batches. It wasn't easy, and things could burn or explode if not monitored closely. He worked hard for his sales, and even those who swore money was no object sought out his brew. It was tough until his sons were old enough to help—but when they grew tall and strong, the business flourished. They learned at the feet of the master brewer. Occasionally, there were some issues with them running off to chase girls or just getting tired of the isolation. They would leave for a few days but always returned willing to embrace the familiarity of the family trade.

Jon realized that at some point each of his sons would return with a woman. It might be tough to find one not so refined as to be put off by their surroundings at the shack. Maybe one or both would leave the business permanently for a mate, but it wasn't likely. The money they had stashed was formidable, but Jon was determined not to appear as being worth much. The less attention he attracted, the better. He got to wondering about the new customers, and his attention was shifted to motion in the distance.

Down the slope, away from the shack, four horses appeared, only three with riders; one would carry the bulk of what was purchased. Jon waited until they were close before he greeted them. Then he approached three young men of average build. Between them they had only one rifle that he could see. One of the men removed his hat and asked, "You Mr. Lewis?"

Two of them spoke in what Jon perceived to be an Irish accent, but not quite. The third was introduced, but Jon didn't catch the name and didn't care, as faces and characters were more important to him. He noted the man's strong, unmistakable French accent and quickly decided he had to be the leader of the three. He appeared to be well spoken and outgoing.

In his business Jon didn't see too many slick characters, as most of his customers were locals, and any well-to-do types who wanted moonshine sent someone on their behalf. They didn't wander up into the hills in their fine clothes and cart home jugs and bottles—unless they didn't want anyone else to know their business.

The three young men looked around the yard and the outside of the shack—the French one was especially observant of everything. But there was nothing to see other than the usual objects belonging to a man living in the woods. They observed Jon's shaggy, unkempt appearance. It was what could be expected—he was a hardened individual of few words.

A few empty pots and tins crusted with food were strewn about, along with some slop buckets not yet disposed of, as there was no outhouse in sight. A three-legged black cat with ragged ears, waiting for a scrap, scooted among old tools and partially chopped felled trees.

There was a woodpile, an ax, and a small fire with a pot of water bubbling. Jon wandered to the fresh meat and skins of the small game and fowl that hung near the smokehouse. He then produced a crude knife, cut a piece of soft rabbit meat from a carcass, and tossed it to the cat.

The smell of sausage smoking in the crudely constructed smokehouse—a combination of pork, onion, and sage—wafted in the air, whetting the men's appetites despite the primitive surroundings. They chatted briefly and then decided that if they finished up their business quickly, they could get to where they were going in daylight.

Something was surfacing in the young Frenchman, who'd been carefully watching Jon. "Do you work alone, Mr. Lewis?" he asked.

"My boys are gone off hunting today." Jon didn't like where this was going and didn't plan to reveal much. There was no need to mention they'd been quarantined in Renfrew's Victoria Hospital with tuberculosis for the last two months. Their mother had succumbed to the disease, and Jon had no idea how he had escaped it. It had been a bad year, but now wasn't the time to let that take over his thoughts.

The procedure wasn't complicated. After determining how much they wanted and the price, he would lead them to a clearing, where they'd wait in plain sight until he came back with the merchandise.

Several things, however, felt somewhat different about this deal: the extra horse and the lack of interest in tasting a sample. They wanted all he could provide that day and didn't haggle with him; they paid top price.

They loaded up, handed over the cash, and left the warm hillside, disappearing into the lush spring forest. He wondered about putting up the next batch a bit early, as he was left dry now.

The next day, Jon prepared his horse with a small cart for a trek to one of the cooking areas, loading up with corn from last year's cold storage, sacks of sugar, and tin boxes of yeast. Startled birds on the slope squawked and circled over the trees lining the trail.

He found the spot and unloaded the materials. A huge copper cooker sat, cold and alone, in the cave. He felt that hopeful wave of anticipation—the smug confidence he felt each time he started a new batch. His brew was renowned and had afforded him actual gold. And no one could find it or even prove that it existed, which made it even finer.

Jon laboriously combined the mash ingredients. He was a bit winded, but that was a side effect of age, he guessed. He coughed away the cloud of whatever was claiming his breath and kept on.

The spring ran past this cook spot, a torrent over slippery shale—fast but not deep, perfect for his purposes. The water had to be fresh, not drawn from sitting pools. He would need to slow down, as the process required him to haul enough water to fill the vat to a certain level. He missed his sons right now; they would have had a contest to see who could move the most water the fastest and laughed until they were sick.

This was one of the more permanent cooking sites. He had built a hearth of stone and mortar, an oven of sorts, under the cooker to contain the fire. It had been cooking for a half hour before he detected the smell he loved; at this stage its aroma was reminiscent of cooked cereal and syrup, but not exactly. It had an earthier, musty smell as it heated up. It wasn't particularly pleasant, but it reminded Jon of success and more money.

Jon admired the clever distilling coils, funnels, and copper tubes. This cooker was his best producer. There were some mathematics and science involved, he understood, but he couldn't be bothered to put a fine point of definition on it, mainly because he couldn't write or read.

He cooked the mash for several hours, hypnotically stirring and using his keen sense of smell to let him know when to put out the fire. He would return later to add the yeast after the liquid had cooled. After methodically inspecting the area for anything conspicuous left behind, Jon made his way back to the shack with his horse and cart.

He opted for a slightly different route this time, a carefully considered alternate approach. The journey through the bush was lush and heady; oppressive humidity paced the activity of every living creature. The hum of insect life and droning bees was pierced by the intermittent call of a crow or hawk as it floated downward from a high-up thermal.

When Jon approached the shack, he saw the French fellow from yesterday, alone and on foot. He was unarmed, he noticed, at least from what he could see. The young man appeared as fine looking and well dressed even though he had been on a bush trail for a couple of days.

Luc was clean shaven and dressed in a fine wool button-down shirt, the color of port wine. "Mr. Lewis, I've been waiting here for a while. I'm here to make another purchase. The brew is good quality, plain and simple."

Jon hesitated. "This isn't a store...and you boys took all I had."

The young man shifted his weight casually and looked off into the distance, thoughtfully, as if crafting a perfect response. "You should consider this opportunity carefully. Not many would pass it up."

Jon wasn't certain what was transpiring. His customer was pleasant enough and seemed to want to arrange to buy up whatever he could and for a better price than what locals could pay.

Depending upon how much Jon could provide, the Frenchman said, he might be able to pay him in advance. They were trying to be more "organized" with the brew in the county, he said. He explained, good-naturedly, that it would benefit everyone involved if they all worked together.

That struck a cold chord in Jon's being. He had heard rumors of situations in which brewers had agreed to certain things and ended up being taken over by one customer. The brewers then only cooked the brew and had no say regarding to whom they would sell. The new middle-positioned party did the selling; sometimes, they even provided the grain, corn, or potatoes, but there would be plenty of pressure to produce.

Jon was listening to what seemed like a solid plan but was hearing something different. He didn't like the proposal. After assessing what might be in his best interest—after all, he was getting older and was on his own now—Jon decided to take a gentle stance with the young man. "I need some time to consider the arrangement," he replied.

With a handsome smile, the young man told him, "Sir, you don't understand. Mr. Tristan Kaye has sent me."

# CHAPTER 5
# THE CRIME LORD

Tristan Kaye hesitated on the top step of Montreal's St. Louis de France Church to survey the street before proceeding inside. The morning had gone well, far transcending that holy place where a spring Sunday morning Mass delivers the soul. For a moment, he didn't want to pass through the entrance and leave the splendor and purity of all he could see outdoors.

Here, in the doorway, he could be moved by the grace of the building and its people, yet not disconnect from the open street and a means of escape, that is, should his private ghosts render him helpless to withstand what he had come to receive. He was grateful that didn't happen too often; he was long past regrets and firmly anchored in his decisions about life. He had been to confession the previous day, and now the resetting of his conscience was complete.

In another lifetime he had been married here. After Madeline's disappearance ten years ago, he'd been entirely convinced he could return to this church, but he'd had to force himself to do so. There was no hard evidence of her death, but he knew in his depths what the situation was; then he took care of it swiftly, cleanly, and as best he could. It was his first encounter with the West End Irish. He then got on with his life.

They had left him alone since then. Once a week he asked for forgiveness in this building, mostly for not being wary enough to have kept her out of harm's way. He never, ever asked to be forgiven for the other.

Tristan loved his city and Sundays, the one day of the week he truly tried not to work, but it didn't always turn out that way; it couldn't be helped. Sundays included his ritualistic visits to his mother's house on Mount Royal Hill for dinner.

His was one of the few automobiles in Montreal, as there were mostly horses and carriages on the street. After the service, his driver, waiting in front of the church, opened the passenger door for him and proceeded to one of the restaurants Tristan owned.

He was meeting a business associate from Rochester, New York.

He didn't consider himself to be actually conducting business on the day of rest, as they were meeting in a public, social environment. Besides, the demand for product in the States was outrageous, and they would need to develop a serious strategy. The Americans could avoid paying the tax if they bought smuggled spirits. The temperance movement was alive and well, and on the Canadian East Coast, prohibition had been voted in. In his opinion, that only served to move people to buy whiskey with a vengeance.

Moving good-quality whiskey and rum wasn't what entirely had made his fortune for him, but in the past year, what his most reliable men had transported had proved lucrative. He had shipped it along the St. Lawrence River to Halifax, where distribution along the US eastern seaboard was mostly a cause for well-disguised vessels and cargo.

Tristan now decided to include another strategy: while still utilizing the St. Lawrence, he also would use other subsidiary rivers, land trails, and more small-time suppliers. If they could load on the north shore of Lake Ontario onto a larger laker that was bound for a port in Monroe County, New York, then the goods could be distributed from Rochester.

This had proved to be a successful method for other distributors, but it had taken him a few years to carefully nurture his relationships with several trail experts, specifically one Algonquin guide from Muskrat Lake, whom he found to be a reliable and amazing aide. Now the time was right to solidify the alliance. He needed these guides to accompany the US-bound shipments on the land leg of the journey through the dense bush and rocky shields. The terrain posed enormous challenges, and Tristan's men stood a greater chance of getting lost without them.

Traveling on the Great Lakes waterways would allow for larger shipments—not as large as shipping from Montreal to Halifax and then to the United States, but it made more sense than moving entirely on land. As the lakes supported bigger vessels, the possible combination of deliveries and ports would be unimaginable. The cargo could be elusive, virtually undetected, and much larger. The provinces had formed a committee to explore that very thing, but Tristan was sure it wasn't for the same purpose he had in mind.

There were excellent depository sites along the St. Marys River and the top of Lake Superior, for instance, and they would have to be well chosen for invisible storage and quick loading at night. If he expanded his suppliers, including even the smallest supplier in Ontario, he could ship via lakers to the farthest US ports on all the Great Lakes.

Previously the liquor had been shipped to the East Coast of Canada already bottled, which had proved tedious at times. Many of his businesses and restaurants already had bottling, packing, and crating facilities in their basements. Bottled cargo was more delicate, and tinkling glass was a dead giveaway when one was trying to pass alcohol off as linens or any basic goods. This new operation would involve mostly large kegs, with bottling to be done at the destinations.

An impressively well-built, dark, masculine figure in a black wool coat and ecru silk ascot, Tristan entered the restaurant. Tristan naturally commanded the attention and respect of others without demanding it. Those who dealt with him were rarely left uncertain as to what his wishes were or where his thoughts were going. His deportment was an asset and well known in his circles. After being seated in the elegant dining room, he ordered a glass of red wine and awaited his associate.

He reflected on how often he and Madeline had dined here or sipped wine casually on the plush velvet salon chairs, as he was doing alone now. He had access to an assortment of female companions, some more virtuous than others and some more appealing than others, yet none were capable of assuaging his loneliness, and as he did in business, he proceeded with caution in his personal life.

The possibility of expansion through Ontario waterways occupied his thoughts. He lit a deeply satisfying cigar to complement his wine. In parts of the country, spirits weren't available, but this was his establishment, and Quebec hadn't conceded to prohibition yet.

His Rochester associate was being escorted to his table—Tom Carter, a highly successful US buyer, who seemed to be alone, which was unusual. After he was seated, the waiter brought them an elegant tray of breads and cheeses. Tristan carried on with the red wine, and Tom ordered a bottle of whiskey, richly amber colored and cold.

"Tom, I'm certain this will be a profitable shift, this inclusion of a partially overland segment. The waterways are being scrutinized heavily now. I can still get the goods out to sea, but this is a new route that can be altered frequently as long as they don't get lost in the back bush." Tristan was watching Tom's face and reactions carefully.

Carter's body language was indicating piqued interest on his part. "I don't much care how it arrives as long as it's good. I've agreed to a relatively small quantity for this first run because I trust your judgment—but I can't agree to a continuation until I see this has gone well. There are risks trekking by land that far to the lake."

"That's where the guides come in. I have seen to it." Tristan was leaning in now, as well.

The two began to formulate a business plan. Tristan decided he needed to see some of the loading and depository sites for himself.

He always had worked from the ground up. "I want to travel to the Great Lakes with a small contingent, including a couple of the new lads who are willing to work hard and look sharp."

The pair he was referring to originated from Canada's East Coast, and prohibition had been voted in on their small island. While originally they'd been on a journey to work on the subsidiary railway through the Ottawa Valley, they had abandoned their path for greater opportunities: making money by using their entrepreneurial skills and not their backs.

Tristan liked the new game plan and welcomed the challenges. The afternoon slipped by, and his presence soon would be required at his mother's home. She was failing physically somewhat and joined him at Mass less frequently. Her spirit and mind, however, were as bright as fire, and even at the age of forty, he didn't relish facing her if he were the slightest bit tardy. She had crossed the Atlantic to be with Tristan after Madeline's disappearance and had mixed feelings about having left her home country of Ireland.

She had made the trip with Tristan's twin brother. Seamus returned to Belfast and the thriving business their father had left them. There was a gold-paved path for them in shipbuilding—ocean liners now—if Tristan had wanted that. He, however, chose to claim the title of "self-made man" and disconnected from the family dynasty. His mother liked to insinuate that Seamus was the civilized one, but Tristan knew his brother occasionally got his hands very dirty, and he had been, in fact, of great assistance when Tristan had settled the score with the West End Irish.

As the meeting wound down, Carter agreed they should meet again in Rochester when Tristan made his inspection trip. Before leaving, Carter had to ask, "How do you stay independent? The West End Irish, the pressure of their growing numbers—surely you feel some connection, being born in Belfast yourself."

Tristan's reply was carefully worded. "I am, first, a businessman and citizen of this city. My being of Irish descent affects my interactions with my family and faith, not my work. My heritage doesn't dictate my choices; sound judgment does." He decided not to share anything further regarding his thoughts on the West End Irish. Carter likely was fishing for information to validate rumors. Tristan concluded straightforwardly, "I have to end our meeting now. I am expected at my mother's for supper."

Carter liked the unsolicited honesty: required at his mother's home. Some men might not have said that. Their hurried departure from the meeting failed to give away the optimistic anticipation of a successful venture—just down the road and across the border.

Independence was Tristan's strong suit, notwithstanding the vulnerabilities Carter pointed out. He knew the gangs were growing powerful, their numbers increasing too. Had his situation with them happened now instead of ten years earlier, when the gangs hadn't been particularly organized, it would have been a much greater challenge.

So far there had been enough business to go around for all, although a few territorial squabbles had required a show of dominance. His network of businesses had expanded so quickly that his staff's numbers rivaled those of the organized gangs.

Tristan loathed that term: *gangs*. Gangs of what? It sounded like a term for unidentified animal life. He was an entrepreneur. He associated with other men of the same stature in society, who referred to themselves as "bosses" or "kingpins."

They definitely defined themselves by their heritage: French, Italian, or Irish, whatever was their lot.

While Tristan adopted none of those titles, he found them more palatable than anything related to the term *gang*. He had worked hard at not getting bought out, and in fact what he did best was persuade smaller businesses to sell out to him; amicable takeovers were his specialty.

His thoughts drifted to the very satisfactory moonshine—from somewhere in the bush in Renfrew County—that the Atlantic lads had brought him. He hoped Luc Boucher was taking care of that situation properly.

Upon reaching his mother's home, he hesitated at this door too. The enormous, luxurious house on the hill reflected her good taste but also her loneliness. She dearly missed his father, long passed and buried in Ireland. His brother, younger by five minutes, was doing well with the family business. But she hadn't really settled entirely on this continent or the one of her birth. Crossing the ocean wasn't unheard of now, especially with their family shipbuilding business. He knew she continually longed to be in both places and sometimes neither.

Siobhan Kaye greeted him eloquently, as usual. "I thought you might have caved into working like a heathen today." She studied his face—that would be the giveaway.

"I was with a client on a social occasion at one of my restaurants. It had to be done," he said, defending himself before it was necessary.

"I should have known. Did you at least go to Mass?" She was relentless.

"Yes. Did you attend today, Mother?" This was a weekly conversation.

"Of course. You know I prefer eleven o'clock to early morning." She moved to another topic. "Do you know your brother's wife is ill? The fourth child has done her in, I think. Four boys...I don't know how she does it—two were almost the death of me." Her eyes held a glint of humor, as Tristan knew full well hers was a good life, somewhat because of her sons. She looked especially young today for her seventy-five years, vibrant and healthy. Immaculate silver hair, swept up elegantly, framed a still regal face, which still commanded reverence. Her occasionally frail-appearing frame sometimes concerned him, as the odd bout of stiffness and lessened mobility hardly brought out the good humor in her. He didn't see her ire too often these days, however, which suited him.

"Have you considered a trip home soon, to see for ourselves how Seamus and his brood are faring? He worships you, and now with your being alone, it may be time to go back." She knew what his response would be.

"Not particularly interested right now," Tristan said. "I've started a new venture, and while I have reputable staff, I want to see the genesis and progress for myself."

"Are you afraid you'll be tempted to stay in Belfast?"

She was going in a direction that made no sense in Tristan's mind, so he changed the topic. "What's for dinner? Hopefully a new conversation is on the menu." That wouldn't go over well, but he couldn't help it.

"Hopefully some basic consideration for one's mother is an option." Siobhan was standing now. Her dress was electric-blue velvet, like her eyes, which were snapping.

"Let's enjoy our dinner, Mother, and not argue."

She sighed and gave her next comment some consideration. "Of course I realize you aren't wanting to make a trip home now, and that the reasons I mentioned are just my way of avoiding my own truths. Simply, I am missing Ireland, and I don't want to make the journey alone. I am feeling vulnerable—not old, Tristan, just vulnerable when it comes to a transatlantic voyage. Is that unreasonable?"

Tristan was caught off guard by her passive tone. He had to admit to himself he was putting off the truth of her missing her home—her empire, really. This had to wait, as usual.

One of the dinner attendants brought an assortment of white wine, so he knew the main course was fowl or fish. He neglected to mention he had started the afternoon with some delicious red during his work meeting.

His well-mannered mother now made an effort to speak French, especially to the French-speaking house staff. Tristan admired her tenacity and her innate love and appreciation of various cultures.

He considered her idea, the elephant in the room, making a journey to Belfast. Not weighing in the contender of basic homesickness, how would he be sure his businesses were run effectively if he gave in and agreed to go? He knew what was coming next. The discussion would revolve around his late father and how he had poured his soul and last breath into the business.

For more than one reason, Tristan found himself wishing he had more of the distilled brew from the hills of Renfrew County.

# CHAPTER 6
# THE ATLANTIC LADS

Malcolm Rast and Stuart Sheen kept tightly to each other, not out of admiration but more, perhaps, from an adherence to the theory of keeping one's competition under a close watch. Knowing their potential enemy was how they survived.

They came from harsh Atlantic poverty, childhood comrades on the unforgiving East Coast, the most eastern part of Prince Edward Island. Most of their friends and family never had never once left the island in their lifetimes.

It was a fine life for some, those who had old money and seaside estates and attended horse races. Their lives, however, had lain in glaring contrast to such things. Each of their families had lived in seaside shanties and resorted to eating horsemeat when necessary. Rast's father sometimes made a sad joke of it with his family: "We're needing a change from damn fish and potatoes."

Summertime on the island was deceitfully pretty, with its salty air and fishing boats and tiny pastel-colored houses. There were barefoot children on the beach. As very young boys, Malcolm and Stuart were those children on the beach. Things changed, however, when they each reached age eleven and were considered old enough to work at hard labor. There was no hesitation on the part of the young lads' fathers. That's when all boys were sent to work.

Springtime meant there were potatoes to plant and fields to work. If their fathers deemed there would be more money made in laboring in the fish plant, waist deep in whatever was caught, then Malcolm and Stuart worked until the last boat was unloaded. All they earned went to their families' general revenue.

Fall brought potato-harvest work, and although automation was evolving, the farmers they worked for couldn't afford that. Some of the jobs didn't even pay cash, only sacks of potatoes for their families, hauled home in the coldness of fall. They were stored in root cellars, to be boiled all winter and served with fish.

By the late fall of the year they turned sixteen, they were old enough to work on lobster and crab boats. The freezing seas always resulted in at least one crew member coming down with pneumonia or sustaining an injury that never allowed him to lead a normal life afterward.

When Malcolm and Stuart turned seventeen, they decided it was time to leave the island. Some fishing-boat crews had come from New York and offered them part-time jobs paying more than hard labor did. The newcomers were self-assured young Americans who smoked manufactured cigarettes and had been places. They invited the two young men to travel to the west side of the island with them and assist in a "job," which mostly involved transporting crated bottled cargo and doing a bit of unloading at the destination.

That was the catalyst that had propelled them away from the island—the beginning of their hungry, westward quest for anything but where they'd come from. Transporting brew as small-time runners occasionally connected them to bigger jobs. Their story was always the same, if they were asked: they were heading west, looking for work on the railway.

They were a smooth duo. They had grown up knowing each other's thoughts and rarely needed to speak their minds to each other. The clever façade came easily to them. They learned early how to work as a team, sometimes communicating with mere glances. Though quiet while alone, they learned the value of engaging folks in people-pleasing stories and conversation. They mastered the art of putting people at ease with easy conversation, lulling them into trust-filled trances and gaining their confidence. Most times, before their true intentions were revealed, a load might be left innocently unattended, or maybe a trusting new acquaintance would pass out from too much rum over an evening of camaraderie, leaving his watch and wallet for the taking. They incorporated their charm into their daily routine with society and reaped the benefits.

Rast, the more vocal of the two, usually led the setup conversations, and Sheen followed, as if the pair were dancing seamlessly together. An ale- and rum-soaked evening in a rowdy pub in Halifax, made perfect with a newly found drunken companion, turned suddenly, as it often did, into an emotional transcendence—the rage and belligerence just beneath the surface. The hostility and pain that had been carefully planted in childhood, nurtured through every season of their young lives, now came to live solidly just under the skin.

"You boys seem to know each other pretty good," the new acquaintance ventured.

Rast and Sheen put down their ale, oblivious now to the lively fiddle music, singing, and laughter around them.

"We are like brothers, friend." Rast steadied himself.

"Are you sure it isn't more than that?" the stranger slurred. He was beyond feeling any inhibitions.

Sheen was on his feet first. "Now you've got our attention." He looked toward Rast.

The stranger continued. "Don't think I am confused...I understand your way—I am hoping you will join me for a drink at my house now. It's getting too late to drink here and...I understand..." His words were fading, all his concentration set on lurching toward the exit.

No words were exchanged between them, just a glance. Rast was first behind him to the door, and Sheen followed. Once in the street, Sheen shoved the man into the dark entrance of the closest alley. Before he could right himself from the second push to the ground by Rast, Sheen had lined up his heavy work boot and repeatedly kicked the stranger in the chest and head. When they saw the blood trickle from a gaping mouth, looking black in the pale night light, they continued down the alley to another tavern. Completely affronted, they didn't even take his wad of cash.

During their second year away, Halifax was the hub of their work. They waited for the shipments to come via carts, trucks, or small boats and loaded them at night onto vessels headed for the US coast. It was the starting point of the flow of spirits throughout the northeast.

There was no shortage of rum from the islands and whiskey from across the ocean. They were at the heart of the transporting, and the city was big enough to create a serious demand, but that wasn't their job. Their job was to get it moving to the United States.

In this industry there were hundreds like themselves, new and eager. The higher-ups noticed who was doing his job well, but they were unpredictable; they could show up at a point of exchange or warehouse without warning. They were men in dark wool suits, usually flanked by a contingent of underlings carrying sleek weapons. Malcolm and Stuart yearned to work their way up the chain and do more organizing and less labor.

They were gunning for more with their new boss, who possessed a long reach. The latest job was distributing whiskey from the United Kingdom—Scotland mostly, and in fact some of the product was referred to as "Scotch." A few, select men unloaded port wine, brandy, and French champagne.

The unloading was the unbelievable part; never had they dared dream of entering a transatlantic ocean liner. They received the go-ahead once all passengers had disembarked and the documented cargo had been unloaded. They understood the reality of this dock world and knew they would lose their lives if they ever spoke of it to anyone.

Rumor had it that there was a new venture, within the country. The aim was to get as much good brew from Ontario down to the top of Lake Ontario and across to the United States, over land that was treacherous, as the roads and trails were crude. There would be guides for the trips, men who grew up locally and specialized in trails and tracking.

Rast was enthusiastic. "We need to get in on this; it's our ticket."

Sheen, a little hesitant to fare the bush trail, said, "We've never gone on horseback for days or weeks. We've done harder things, but do you think we can make this go?"

"Do you want to stay here? I'm going. Do what you want." Rast knew this would light a fire under his friend. He sometimes needed the push. "The boss has the connections; he has the bloody ships for crossing, for Christ's sake. He probably likes lads like us, growing up by the sea and all."

"You always think I want the same as you—that I can't think for myself. Why are you like that?" Sheen was feeling like he was being steered.

"I am like that because you can't think for yourself—it's true," Rast said impatiently.

"And you're an arse." Sheen was defeated.

"I might be. And I'm also not going to be a runner all my life. I'm going to get in on a good job. You are too if you just pay attention and keep on like we are." Rast lit two cigarettes and passed one to his friend.

"We've been in the muck long enough."

# CHAPTER 7
# THE LOST SOUL

Allowing the satisfaction derived from the perfectly fitted shoe to briefly ease his nagging angst, Josef spoke quietly to the horse, leaned down to inspect his effort one last time after the walk, and then stood up straight to stretch his stiff back and listen—which was more like sensing than listening. The barely audible steps seemed purposeful yet strangely impeded in a manner that, if he let his good intuition speak, might be telling of a lost soul approaching. Today he didn't want his intuition to speak.

Darkness chilled the evening air as Josef put the horse away in the stable. Maxwell likely would stop by tomorrow to retrieve the animal. As he was a good customer and friend, Josef looked forward to seeing him. Neither could rationalize the altercation with the German fellow, having debated it thoroughly when he'd brought the horse to the shop.

Josef hesitated at the iron garden gate that leaned against the wall; it was for Giselle—an ornate gift he had worked on for a few weeks. It was finished and ready to present to her for their anniversary. They would share a meal of their favorite dishes tomorrow evening: stuffed wild grouse Josef had hunted, apples and onions fried together, and steamed potatoes. This would all be topped off with apple pie with slices of aged cheddar. Thinking about it made his stomach growl, and he hurried to get to the house for tonight's supper.

His thoughts of tomorrow were interrupted by a shrill voice calling out—something indistinct, not a woman's voice exactly, but if it were a man's, then the man was extremely distressed.

With a red face, he emerged from the shadows on the road toward Josef, veering as he approached. He spoke very quickly, with words Josef couldn't comprehend, and seemed very agitated, possibly drunk.

He was shouting, "You want the farmers to bow before the businessman? And wait to be slaughtered like swine?" He was waving his arms and appeared to be past rational thinking.

Josef had no clue what he was alluding to and told him to stop where he was and to speak slowly. Then he recognized the face. It was the farmer, Ivan Hauffe, from the altercation with Maxwell. Facts formed instantly in his racing mind: a recently landed—two years recently landed—German immigrant who farmed a few miles away.

There had been talk of how ill-tempered and excitable he was, always thinking he was being slighted at every turn. Was there a family? Yes, a wife and two sons, and none of them spoke English very well. There also were rumors of hunger and violence within the home.

Josef's attempt to calm him with a likewise demeanor failed. "Calm down, man! Listen to what I'm telling you. I don't understand."

Hauffe either wasn't listening or understanding. He headed into Josef's shop, grabbed the large forging tongs, and pushed past him toward the stable. Josef ran to follow Hauffe, even though he cringed thinking of what might happen in a confined area with the man. Once inside the stable, Hauffe exchanged the tongs for a riding whip. Then he reached the newly shoed horse and drew back dramatically.

Josef's memory took him back to the incident in front of the gristmill—Maxwell on horseback, arguing heatedly with Hauffe. It didn't matter what it was about; he wasn't about to let anyone attack him with a whip or harm a horse in his charge. What was the farmer's intent? Now mentally prepared for a second physical altercation, he lunged at the farmer's legs and knocked him over.

The pair struggled and rolled, and when the farmer was still, Josef awkwardly tried to stand, looking to find some rope. He needed to tie him up until he could get help. Josef was staggering, unable to right himself, and didn't see Hauffe recover and get to his feet. As quickly as he had appeared, he grabbed the large forging tongs and brought them down full force on Josef's skull.

He hit the ground facedown and aware of a glowing vision, in detail: a wonderful moment, the presenting of Giselle with the lovingly handcrafted anniversary gift. She was beaming and elated to receive it. With this, he slipped away.

Hauffe leaped up as if to bolt and then froze on the spot, suspended briefly like a marionette, before he collapsed. He heard the approaching footsteps—running, a man shouting—but it wasn't the right man, and now all had been seen.

# CHAPTER 8
# THE WIDOW

Giselle Boucher Reicher hadn't questioned her husband's abilities, beliefs, or even his disinterest in breaking the land. They passively, almost unknowingly, had formed an unspoken agreement. She understood how much he had wanted at least one son to keep his craft alive, and he had known she had seen the ever-increasing fragility of his life's work. Yet they hadn't shown each other disappointment; that was just the way it was.

Her spirit was her strength, and her two daughters, Marie and Elise, were her life—her present life's breath. Her past life, across the St. Lawrence, was still with her of course; when she was a small child, her values had been instilled there in the crowded three-room house.

It really wasn't a proper house—more of a reinforced shack with faux walls, flimsy cloth or wood partitions substituting for real walls. Why did anyone build such minuscule structures to begin with? She remembered the freezing temperatures, even with a fire burning and six of them in total. She recalled never feeling warm, especially at night, unless it was July; the winters were beyond bitter.

Constantly exhausted and sad, her mother seldom spoke. Always there was a sick child, coughing relentlessly until he or she succumbed or passed the illness on to a sibling.

But there was the faith; her mother and father believed that was their lifeblood, and Mother Mary would be there for them and the two small babies in the graves on the riverbank. Giselle thought of the little white crosses, and the image almost comforted her. Something had to ease the sting of the last few days' events; the present was pulling her back from her daydream of childhood. The chilliness was definitely here in the present as well.

It seemed as if it had occurred in slow motion: the hysterical revelation of Josef's violent death in the stable. Why hadn't she gone to check on him and tell him to come in for supper? She may have been able to prevent what had happened. She endured the steady flow of people coming to her house to see her and her daughters; her girls were numb and wide eyed the entire time.

On his way to see Josef, Will had found the farmer, stumbling, outside of the stable. With Josef's bleeding and lifeless body nearby, he surmised the carnage without difficulty. He dragged Hauffe off his feet, trussing him with leather reigns hanging on the wall. The farmer was mumbling and incoherent. He resisted nothing physical but wouldn't answer Will, who was shouting for answers. Will ran to the door of the house, wondering if Josef's wife and daughters were harmed. He found Giselle immediately and, while shielding her from the scene, explained what had happened in the stable.

To keep herself steady, she brought her mind around to more routine thoughts. Would her sister and two brothers journey to see her once they received the news? Her sister had married within ten miles of their family homestead and had three children. As bright as Giselle, Aline had convinced her husband to take them to Montreal and settle there—away from her roots. Giselle's brothers had also headed for Montreal. Stephan, the eldest brother, settled down along the St. Lawrence, a successful farmer raising a family.

Giselle, along with Josef and their girls, had traveled to see them once a year. Each time, a debate, concerning breaking the hilly Ontario land versus holding on to a dying family trade, lasted the entire visit. On the journey home, she would say to Josef, "You can't dismiss the concept entirely. People will gravitate to automation, and where will that leave you? Maybe we should get some land."

Josef would shrug and nod, and that would be the end of it.

Luc, now twenty-three, the youngest of her siblings, wasn't in a hurry to relive his childhood. He was clever and good looking, wanted a high life, and had a worldly air about him with an unexplainable genesis. He was elusive, writing to Giselle randomly and unexpectedly from various locations in the valley and sometimes Montreal. His letters were intelligent, vibrant, and hopeful; he carried no pessimisms from their childhood. He worked at various jobs that, in Giselle's mind, didn't exactly correlate to how he always had money.

Marie and Elise always were excited to hear from their uncle and receive his gifts. He loved life and wasn't about to die of pneumonia in a freezing shack in Quebec like their parents. Giselle felt the same. She couldn't escape wanting her daughters to keep the faith with her, so she'd had them baptized, and they attended church every Sunday, often without Josef.

Josef would attend if he could tear himself away from his work. He didn't care if it was the Sabbath— if there were things to tend in the shop, he remained behind. Giselle didn't insist, as she questioned many things about her faith on her own terms. She may not have vocalized them, but the doubts were there. She knew some things made no sense to her—having more children than a couple could take care of was one of them.

She never had spoken of intentionally stopping at two children, even without their having a son. She wouldn't bring that with her from the past. The will of God could be damned in this case.

She pulled her black shawl around her more tightly and felt the presence of her younger girl, Marie, wanting to comfort her mother and to be comforted; soon the older one, Elise, joined silently. Sitting together before the evening fire, they quietly absorbed the household's new three-person dynamic, remaining a family of four that was missing one member. They would bury Josef tomorrow and face the enormous changes in their lives together as soon as the last shovelful of dirt was tossed.

# CHAPTER 9
# THE PRIEST

A warm, comforting breeze accompanied Father Gaston through the cemetery as he walked lightly and assuredly among the headstones. He was performing his routine check of the grave site. The sound of the nearby Helle usually numbed the souls who came here to cry, and for that he was grateful.

He wondered about the souls who remained here. Seldom did he feel chilled or uncomfortable among the resting deceased. He felt less comfortable among the grieving, living souls, however. He never knew what to expect with them. On an off day, coping with the hysteria could be downright frustrating.

Father Gaston's congregation believed him to be powerfully strong and gifted with the lost souls and

suffering lambs of God. His community was changing, however, and this last loss of life was particularly
mysterious and disturbing. He was no stranger to losing them too soon; that part he could situate properly. It was the lack of explanation and reason that
troubled him.

There was no obvious connection between the
two—the farmer and the blacksmith. He needed to
link them somehow, if only to make the service make
sense to the villagers in some way. He always used the
truth to comfort mourners; it was a direct route to
their rationalizing what had happened and keeping
things in perspective. They didn't need to know that
his telling the truth was mostly for his selfish, personal motives. They didn't need to know he practically
loathed comforting them sometimes.

The police had talked to Father Gaston; they
always did. With every unnatural death came questions, just in case the priest could shed some light
on any confession issues. They knew he was bound
by his oath to go to them if he learned anything seriously incriminating, but they still had to probe. The
other promise and oath prevented him from reveal-
ing their inner truths. It was so complex.

As Josef usually didn't attend Mass, Father Gaston
had nothing to report. Mrs. Reicher frequently
attended with her daughters and never seemed

uncomfortable with that arrangement. *Rather inde-pendent of her,* he thought, but he secretly admired her for that. She had always just marched in with the children and took her place to worship without him by her side.

The headiness of the vines and blossoms decorating the headstones was almost sickening. He stood alone among the perfectly positioned figures of stone and concrete. There were crosses, angels, and no shortage of cherubs. What really made people inscribe such similarly bland phrases? Why didn't some of them write—for all eternity to witness—that they were thanking God it was over for some of these souls, for their own sake and that of the deceased's?

Father Gaston's congregation would never suspect him of these dreaded thoughts. Smiling inwardly, he lingered over the gash in the ground. Soon all eyes would be on him. He didn't struggle with hubris; in fact, he believed it kept him buoyant. And the flock cooperated with him in a fine, codependent manner.

His mind drifted back to his childhood and early adult years in Montreal. The shipyards along the St. Lawrence had beckoned him when he was a curious child, and like other children, he spent time in fascination there. He couldn't have known then, but when certain things transpired later in his life, he was certain that God had all but illuminated them for him as a youngster. Such a coincidence it was, where he ended up.

But in the present, it was very difficult to find light to help him understand some things. Certain members of his flock left him feeling cold and bewildered. It had to be acknowledged—he had to speak a prayer more often for them. Perhaps, he concluded, they assumed that he didn't observe them while he was delivering a sermon, that he was so enraptured with his speech about the Lord that he didn't notice when they had lost interest and tried to amuse themselves.

Father Gaston, however, easily noticed when they grew disinterested in salvation and knew where their thoughts and attention were turning. Something as simple as boredom spoke a million words to what was going on inside them. He knew this for certain; a person's true essence was never very far away.

# CHAPTER 10
# GRAVESIDE

E ven though it was only noon, Giselle consumed a glass of red wine, before then dressing in her best black and taking her place in the church. Some kind of unseen warmth and surreal aura cocooned her through her hours of sadness. Marie and Elise stood closely on either side of her. She looked around at the people with her: some as sad as she, others gripped with the fragility of their own mortality, and others who were, quite simply, hoping to glean information.

She noticed the police presence and never imagined their involvement would be part of losing her husband. She sometimes had worried that Josef worked too hard and might succumb to coronary stress—but murdered at their home, here in Loren?

The police had come to the house, in uniform, respectful but still looking at her as if she were guilty of something. They pressed her for any knowledge of Josef's relationship with Hauffe. She knew nothing; there had been no previous conversation in their home about the farmer.

The officers found this unsatisfactory and asked to examine the account books. How could such a violent attack be provoked for no reason? They were hell-bent on finding a disagreement about services rendered and payment, perhaps. There were no records of Josef having had any business with Hauffe.

More than once, the authorities asked whether she'd had any relationship or interactions with the man. Giselle couldn't fathom where this inquiry was going and responded honestly. What was the point of asking the same question in a slightly different way several times? She saw through the basic interrogation technique and patiently waited for the conclusion. They also tried asking her the same questions in various areas of her home and then, of course, the stable. It shook her, and she couldn't hide her pain, as she had been avoiding the stable. They didn't allow her to let the girls wait in another area and seemed curious about their reactions to the questions posed to their mother.

Then, as quickly as the officers had appeared, it was determined the interview was over. "If you happen to remember anything, please contact us," one of them told her before the officers exited her home.

She had closed the door and steadied herself; she needed to return to her clear and present concerns. She was beginning to worry about administrative matters: the business, Josef's death documents, his will. *Are the accounts in order?* she wondered. She made a mental note to make appointments with the banker and the solicitor. Giselle anticipated the strange and varied reactions of the people in Renfrew County, who had heard everything, miraculously, over the past few days.

Josef didn't always attend church with his family, which she tried to make light of when it was pointed out. It didn't come between the two of them as husband and wife, so why should others care? Father Gaston never chastised them but clearly was disappointed. After the funeral, he would be a great comfort and advisor if he maintained a gentle persona. Giselle wouldn't consider entertaining any strong views about how the church thought she should conduct herself from here forward.

That afternoon their house was filled with mourners, friends and neighbors alike. She couldn't fault her siblings for not being able to attend. Their families and lives couldn't be uprooted on such short notice to make the journey to the village.

Giselle could imagine Aline appearing on a subsequent, unexpected day, in a wave of strength and comfort, giving all of herself to her sister and nieces. But where was Luc? She had held hope that his nomadic lifestyle would have him nearby, just for her. Josef had thought her young brother was in the valley—what was it he'd mentioned? It wasn't coming to her now.

Giselle had managed to hover above the whole graveside ordeal, imagining herself as a circling falcon, silent and never touching down to the ground to be a part of it. Deep breaths kept her calm; she saved the agonizing tears for later, when she was alone.

She pushed past the people in her kitchen: well-meaning souls, staring at her as though she might self-combust. She went through to the veranda, which surrounded the house. Finding a garden chair, sinking down into it, and then looking as far into the distance as possible, she focused on the trees and the birds flitting in them.

Father Gaston followed and sat quietly with her, the two of them observing the delicate greenery of springtime. For a moment they were oblivious to her plight at hand.

After some minutes of comforting, reverent silence, Father Gaston finally spoke. "My dear, it won't be easy. You'll be scrutinized for being alone and in need and even more so if you aren't alone and are self-sufficient."

What was he getting at? Giselle was preparing to give his statement further consideration and a reply when she heard Luc's voice in the kitchen. She rose to head that direction. He hadn't yet encountered his nieces and rushed to his sister's side. They exchanged a quick greeting and embrace, each anxious to assess the other's emotional condition.

"How did you hear? I had no idea how to reach you," Giselle exhaled.

"It was by chance. I was a couple days away from here, there was some talk in another village about a death, a brutal killing actually"—he looked down— "and I knew it was Josef." He stiffened and suppressed the grief and pain for his sister. Her stoicism was almost shocking.

He requested a private conversation with his sister from the priest and then gazed into the distance when they were alone; it was a family trait, to think before speaking. From his coat he produced a bottle of what he described as very decent whiskey for them to steady themselves. Then Luc finally asked Giselle to tell him exactly, in detail, what she knew of the murder of her husband.

"You can't leave anything out, Giselle. I see you are even-keeled right now. Can you do it?" he pressed her.

"I don't have a lot of information. He was working in his shop, as usual, a bit late, nothing serious. I had sent Elise to the stable to remind him about supper. She came back immediately and said he was to be not long." She looked at Luc as if seeking something. "Then the sound of Will hammering on the door— he sat me down, told the girls to not move, locked the front door, and used the phone. There was difficulty with the line, but he called the authorities. He then told us Josef had been…attacked"—she looked away—"and that there was no hope."

Luc pulled her focus back. "Nothing to share about that farmer? What did Will or whatever his name is say? Do you know of him?"

"Nothing. Will said he was incoherent and didn't seem adverse to be taken into custody. I think he and his family arrived from overseas, Germany maybe, a few years ago. They are struggling on a farm somewhere around Loren. Will says he has heard that the man is volatile and unpredictable. I believe him to be insane…What else should I think? I should hate him, Luc." She withdrew—but only for a moment. "What can be done about it anyway? There will be a trial—a trial but no real answers."

Giselle sobbed uncontrollably for a minute that seemed like an hour to her brother. As she focused and composed herself, it occurred to her that no matter how carefully she approached her life from this day forward, she would be judged, regardless of the truth.

# CHAPTER 11
# THE FARMER'S SON

Will Frank pondered when and how he could speak with his best friend's widow. His world had been altered immeasurably. Several days after the murder, he was still reeling, having discovered Josef's lifeless body and the stunned, incomprehensible Hauffe.

It wasn't difficult to surmise what had transpired; the farmer was still holding the weapon, seemed spent, and didn't attempt to escape.

Will had spent hours trying to work out the reason for the murder. It was nothing but an ugly, unbearable twist for Josef's family and friends during an otherwise beautiful spring. The thought of the discovery and apprehension was branding his memory with overwhelming revulsion, but that wasn't what was concerning him today. It was hearing the farmer's son Ivan outside the holding cell, where his father was carrying on in German. Will understood the language, even though his family hadn't spoken it publicly for two generations—only in private, as his father had kept on about embracing the language of their new country, saying it would be better for business.

Before he had entered the town jailhouse, he had debated whether to do so. What was there to be gained? He couldn't resist the desire to corner the man and demand an explanation. That was not really an option with the jailers on duty—of course, he wouldn't. But he could certainly visualize Hauffe succumbing to his insistence and then his racing to Giselle with it all. He could be the one to explain it all to her.

Uncertain what he would say to Hauffe, he stopped short, around the last hallway corner, as he heard young Ivan's voice. Not fully aware of his surroundings, Will was startled by a security guard. "Hey, Will, what could you want in this place?" the man asked. They knew each other, as Will had sold him harnesses on several occasions.

"I wanted to see for myself, you know..." Will didn't know how to explain his feelings.

"I have to say I'm surprised to see you here, being that you found Reicher and all—you can't talk to this guy, you know, you being a witness in the crime," the jailer explained gently. "Now it's OK for the son to visit him—I think they are having a go at the powers that be. They speak the German, and that's OK by me as I don't want to know anything, if you get my meaning. That's the older lad—he is about twenty. The younger one is likely at home with the mother, trying to sort things out and the like." The jailer liked to talk. "Anyway, since you're here, can you sit in my chair for a few minutes until I get back from relieving myself? It's a long day here sometimes."

It was Providence. He couldn't say anything to the farmer, but he could listen. "You go ahead—no rush. I'll just sit here." Will was satisfied with what transpired.

He decided that listening might be better than speaking, anyway. No point in getting on the wrong side of the son.

The jailer went the opposite direction of the holding cells and through a steel door with a key. Will noted he did not lock it from the other side. All the while they had been chatting, the voices from down the hall were starting to rise and quicken.

Young Ivan sounded furious. "You did what you had to, Father! It's not your fault. Any man would have agreed to it." What was he meaning? Then Will heard Ivan agreeing with his father that it all had been Josef's fault.

Hauffe's voice was raspy and emotional. "I have seen the worst in men, banding together against foreigners, wanting to be rid of us, and the blacksmith had the hatred—for our own safety, I had to put him down." He continued to explain to his son that he would tell the authorities Josef had baited him, goading him into a fight; maybe that would spare him a death sentence.

Will listened intently but could barely hear now—his blood pounding in his ears. There was no hatred on Josef's part and certainly no reason for anyone to fear him. And his good friend did not hate immigrants. Did Hauffe really think using that angle with his son would hide his murdering spirit, would justify what had happened?

Father and son vehemently maintained that Josef should have had nothing to do with the mayor, let alone service his horse. The mayor was a hater too.

The humiliating argument in front of the gristmill had disgraced him publicly, Hauffe insisted. The mayor wouldn't even dismount to talk to Ivan on level ground; his behavior was unforgivable. Maxwell Loren couldn't understand where the conversation was going and had insisted, in a sarcastic, exasperated manner, that Hauffe brush up on his command of English; he said he wasn't making an effort and spoke like a child.

It was unthinkable that someone in the mayor's esteemed position was taunting Hauffe for his poor English. Their family wouldn't let that pass, Hauffe and young Ivan agreed. They conversed passionately, and then, suddenly, without making an obvious shift, the two spoke seriously in guttural, barely audible tones. Hauffe was telling his son something important, but Will could make out only snippets. What he heard clearly was young Ivan's promise to his father—who was sobbing in as hushed tones as possible, intermittently—that he would get everything sorted out.

Will was aware that his murdered friend had witnessed the altercation and had interfered, with the intent to mediate. Somehow Hauffe had misinterpreted his actions as aggression and threats. That easily enough could have happened, but surely the volatile Hauffe didn't assume Josef should shun Maxwell, his good friend and customer.

To take a life over an insult to one's pride? Possibly the Hauffes were a different sort; no one in the community knew the family well. How far would they take the vendetta? Should Will warn Giselle? Of course he should, but when and how?

The Hauffe farm wasn't more than two miles from the Reicher property. Was young Ivan as volatile as his father? Likely this was all talk to pacify Hauffe, who could be facing a death sentence in short order.

Giselle's worries were enormous now and, at the moment, Will didn't want to deliver to her the possibility of having to be wary of the rage-filled son. Perhaps young Ivan's stance would soften, and in time he would understand his father hadn't been the victim.

Will would keep an eye on the situation and not trouble his best friend's widow with this information right now. He focused on what lay ahead, in the days after burying Josef. He hoped he never would encounter the Hauffe family, but it was a certainty; his was a small village, as was the valley.

He decided not to confront the farmer in the jail cell, especially as he heard deliberate footsteps approach from the other direction. Were they footsteps of authority? Perhaps it was the jailer; perhaps, a local citizen wanting to see the crazy monster in the cage. Whoever approached elicited a strong reaction from Hauffe.

The shouting was deafening, and was that laughter from the visitor? Will headed for the door the jailer had exited from to find him. The raised voice of the farmer sickened him, as it brought his mind back to the somewhat blurry memory of his discovery of Josef's body.

The jailer came back through the door before Will reached it. "What the hell is the racket? Who is in there? I must not have locked the other door."

"No one came by me," Will offered. As the jailer strode by to sort out the situation, Will decided he had seen and heard enough, as it would be a long day's think to understand the words of the Hauffes.

The farmer's voice also reminded him of the burial and his sad attempt to support Giselle and her daughters through it. He hadn't done an adequate job; their strength overshadowed the sickened, cold pit in his being that should have been bravery. Will wanted nothing more than to be the man they took solace from, but even one empty, white, innocuous glance from Giselle caused him to shrink.

# CHAPTER 12
# PEMBROKE COURTROOM

"He appears to be in another world." Will leaned into Giselle, hoping to be helpful. She had no response and barely any thoughts of anything aside from an eventual speedy exit from the building. Approximately seventy people occupied the main courtroom of the Renfrew County courthouse in Pembroke. The attractive, gleaming wooden benches were perfectly aligned in the sturdy stone walls, and with its high windows, the room could have passed for a place of worship, complete with serious souls—their heads lifted upward and forward, almost unwillingly—drawn into the agonizing proceedings.

It wouldn't be as slow as most trials, with no looming uncertainty of guilt or the possibility of convicting an innocent person.

In one of the cells, the farmer slumped, awaiting the inevitable. His usual angry edginess was snuffed and smoldering like a smoky fire in rain.

Giselle opened up unexpectedly. "I imagined him to be larger, stronger, and more frightening looking."

Will stopped breathing and waited for something further from her.

"He looks pitiful. Imagine that I am here, Will, with all these ogling folk and the man who murdered my husband, and all I want to do is run out of here. He never looks around or for me, in particular. I find that odd," she said.

Will found her observations odd. "His guilt is preventing him from facing you." His basic common sense, simple and straightforward, paled next to her intuitive, insightful words.

Hauffe's wife's demeanor was silent and small; the sons', the opposite.

"My father cannot be beat down by your laws!" young Ivan, demonstrative and angry, almost to the point of needing to be removed from the courtroom, shouted. The other one was too young to form his own opinion, an impressionable boy, clearly going with what his older brother had told him: the blacksmith had driven their father to the brink of his dignity, and therefore, he had acted accordingly—harshly but accordingly.

Giselle, unaware of how many hours or days were passing, absorbed the trial benignly, with seemingly little emotion. The jury convened only once; there were no questions, and hardly any discussion took place among its members.

During a break within the confines of the stuffy building, the prosecution lawyer faced her, stiffly sitting in her seat. "The case is an undisputed one-way story, with not a shred of possibility that your husband's death had been anything but cold-blooded murder. The only gray area is the farmer's sanity."

She had no comment.

As Hauffe had no previous social history with the blacksmith—or any interaction with him before the argument on the village street—his mental state was clearly an issue. There had been local witnesses to the argument with the mayor, and they had testified regarding Hauffe's unsettling, unprovoked hostility.

On the stand, Hauffe's subdued self was abandoned; he was rendered incapable of answering questions without displaying complete disregard for courtroom protocol, much less basic social interaction. His ranting and hysteria were there for all to see and judge. When the court addressed him, Hauffe either shouted or mumbled, rocking himself in his chair.

The jury and Justice Harrison interpreted Hauffe's blow to the skull of Josef Reicher, village blacksmith and family man, as nothing but an intention to end his life by homicide and sentenced him accordingly. Giselle and Will listened to the judge's brief recount of the events, the seriousness and the consequences. After stating he had never witnessed a more sense-less and mysterious case, Justice Harrison sentenced Hauffe to death row. He would spend his remaining time in the Kingston Penitentiary, with an order for a mental-health assessment upon admission and pos-sible relocation to the insane ward to await his hang-ing in Gray Tower.

Will's deeply exhaled breath and Giselle's stifled crying simultaneously broke the tight silence in the courtroom, but only for a few seconds before the din of the crowd's response overtook their suddenly small presence.

# CHAPTER 13
# KINGSTON PENITENTIARY

The convict transport truck was loud and jostling. Hauffe had never ridden in an automobile before, let alone a large truck. It didn't sit well with him, the growling monsterlike sound of grinding gears working up to a crescendo of speed.

The truck was transporting four men to the penitentiary, and it would be a few days' drive. The drivers made a few stops along the way, only to briefly relieve themselves or change drivers. All passengers were unceremoniously ill from cold fear and lack of warmth while trying to sleep in the truck's hard seats, sitting up with no pillow.

When the truck was nearing their destination, Hauffe could smell the river. It must be a great one, not like the Helle in his village in Renfrew County, which was nothing like the waters in his home country.

Would that liar find his way here while he was imprisoned? His thoughts had been stilled somewhat on the arduous drive, but they were heatedly coming alive again. Gritting his teeth until his jaw ached, he couldn't keep his rage suppressed. The killing had to happen, of course; he'd been duped and wrongfully taken. There was no other way to see it.

The truck pulled up in front of the institution, looking insignificant on the vast concrete that butted against the stone and brick. Hauffe stumbled off with the others, stiff and aching from days of sitting. Static security officers stood, armed, waiting for them to pass by with the mobile officers escorting them.

"Keep moving! Help yourselves along—don't make us do it! Line up in front of the entrance in an orderly manner!" A guard shouted repeatedly.

"I will be leaving this place!" Hauffe defied his escorts.

"You will be doing as we ask—no more and no less." The guard's voice was becoming more monotone, like a carnival worker calling out the same story night after night.

Hauffe's dialogue was now in German—alternating from pleading to defying. It went without notice while the guards prepared to take them through the admission process.

"Take me out of here!" He was slowly and steadily gaining momentum through his rage, and his hostile shouts weren't well received. Several extra officers appeared.

"We aren't putting up with any rudeness or shouting! Get that into your skull, and you'll get through this, man!"

The explanation and subsequent request wasn't heeded.

"I am waiting here for my son! He knows where to find me! I won't stay!" Hauffe tried to break free of his shackles and knocked another prisoner over, all the while thrashing from side to side on the ground.

"Hold it there and settle yourself! Where is the damn medic?" The guard had lost all patience.

Before Hauffe could glance behind him, one of them thrust a needle into his thigh. Within a minute he was considerably slowed down, and the movement of the group seemed strangely fuzzy and deliberate; four guards stood ahead of Hauffe and three behind. They had gotten him onto his feet again. One guard called out to some others behind a large gate, telling them to unlock it immediately.

Hauffe's confusion nearly paralyzed him. How had he gotten inside this building? Vague memories of a young officer from the Kingston constabulary assisting him onto a bench in the holding cell swirled in his mind—was he imagining them? Why did he feel so weak? What was all the shouting about?

The dim lights and the cold echoes of the institution's harsh sounds were miles from his previous life, one filled with warmth and natural light. Were the voices yelling at him? He heard laughter too. He felt an all-encompassing wave of something wash over his body, and his legs buckled, but he didn't fall; a guard was supporting him on either side now. They were saying things—something about taking him to his permanent cell—but he didn't understand most of it.

He had recent memories of feeling enraged, but why? He knew he'd been angry for days. The guards told him to keep moving forward, and then they shoved him into a cell. He faded into a semi-comatose state while one of the guards removed his shackles and cuffs. Then he was left—for countless hours—unattended.

Hauffe came out of his sleep twelve hours later, faced with the stern voice of another uniformed man. "You'll be given a drink when the rest of the prisoners are." His thirst and headache were all consuming.

A guard stood looking at him from outside the cell but didn't appear particularly concerned.

He was trying to get answers from Hauffe, who responded with garbled shouting. "Speak some English, and we'll all know what you want." He turned to another guard and motioned toward Hauffe. "Can't tell if he's Polish or German or what, but he's carrying on like he's crazy, and the medication is wearing off."

When he panicked, Hauffe didn't understand the words from the guards or the other convicts. He understood only his own voice, and he had to repeat himself continually, as they weren't catching on. They either ignored him or put a hand up for him to stop speaking. Was he to speak of nothing? He sensed the other convicts weren't even attempting to speak to the officers. After several hours of not being able to subdue him or understand him, they left him alone.

"This one will be heading for the tower anyway— just leave him." Futility had set in for the hour.

He had no choice; he had to keep trying; he yelled, cried, and shouted until he had no voice, before he collapsed and finally slipped off into sleep.

# CHAPTER 14
# THE INSANE WARD

When Hauffe awoke, he saw a tin plate of meat mush and bread and a tin mug of water on the floor of his cell. His head was clearer now. As he recalled his panic and hysteria, he decided to keep quiet and listen and observe the others.

A burly guard approached the cell. "You'll stay in here for a few days until you settle down," he said, "and then you can eat with the others."

He saw blankets as well as a crudely constructed frame that served as a bed. But he wasn't lying on them. He was still on the floor next to the food. Then he heard the voice. Thank God! One of them spoke his language and called out to him. Hauffe answered back. He heard! The voice asked what he was doing here in Kingston, on the river, in this prison.

Rising to his feet, Hauffe explained the whole story: the argument, the "accident," and the blur of what had happened since then. He wept while the anonymous voice listened to his story. It told him to be especially quiet right now and not draw attention to himself; his carrying on like this wouldn't work. He explained, carefully, that if others here understood his language, maybe they could help him get home again, and if he kept quiet forever, he might never find them. Although Hauffe was filled with panic, he rocked himself on the wooden bed instead of yelling.

Two weeks later nothing had changed. He hadn't been let out of the cell. Food and drink were placed inside once a day. A guard came daily to remove and replace the waste and wash buckets.

The German voice was fading and rarely called upon him now, and then suddenly it stopped answering him. He faced the high-up, tiny barred window as long as there was light in the small cell.

"I know the truth will come here, to this place, this hell for me." Hauffe held fast.

He waited each day. Then, when darkness finally came, he stretched and moved to stop the pain of aching stiffness in his limbs and joints. Being a farmer, he knew that long periods of inactivity could bring on more pain even than intense labor, and he felt best when he did some of both.

But he didn't speak or move in the daylight for fear of drawing attention to himself, as the voice had advised. He learned how to suppress his desire to scream. The faceless voice was receding and asking him to come along to a more peaceful place.

How would he do it? How could he end his own life in this place? He must make sure he had a solid plan because he didn't want to be found and revived to serve out his days until hanged in the tower. He wouldn't give them that satisfaction.

This was a place of humiliation and cruelty, and he didn't belong here. How dare they take away his ability to run his own life? In the outside world, on more than one continent of the world, he had bowed to no man—not even God.

Hauffe knew he had the fortitude to starve to death, but how much more suffering should he have to endure? If he could ask some of the others, it could help. Would any of them understand him? They mostly seemed to look confused about him or outwardly taunted him. They made circular gestures with a forefinger around the sides of their heads to one another and laughed loudly. What did that mean?

Some days, he was taken out to the yard, marched with the others to the rock quarry to labor all day long. Although the lime and shale were foreign substances to him, the harder he shoveled, the better he felt.

The first two days in the quarry did not go well, as his ferocity with the shovel went beyond their wishes. He raged against the rock, flailing dangerously close to fellow prisoners with the provided tools. And no amount of warnings could stop him. Smashing the shovel and pick against the rock soothed his soul. And for his efforts, much to his confusion, he was tied to a cart, unable to move, until the workday was over for the others. They said it was for everyone's safety.

On the third day, he tried his best not to be over-zealous, which made things worse. He could feel his desire to gouge the rock surfacing again. He didn't want to be stopped—the rage had to come out, but this prison kept it beat down. He was drawing the attention of the guards again.

"He's in a state again and holding us up," one observed to another officer. "Hey there, Hauffe, quiet yourself or there will be a lashing!"

He was slipping into panic again. The only other thing Hauffe could do to better his situation was to find the money he was promised; he was certain it was hidden in the limestone. He repeatedly asked everyone around him to watch for it. Had they found it yet? Was he shouting again? He must get his point across somehow. Why were the prisoners and guards staring?

Now the warden and a mental-health doctor were on horseback, observing him, while he was yet again tied to a horse cart. He yelled at everyone and finally lost his voice.

The warden at first had suggested the wooden box. Hauffe had seen it; it wasn't much bigger than a coffin. But then the mental-health doctor decided sedation was necessary. So the dreamy state was induced after buckets of cold water were thrown on him because he smelled bad.

Back in his cell, Hauffe listened to the voice; it had returned to him, and it was beautiful.

Then, unexpectedly, fate showed him some more compassion, helping him with his plan. Out of the blue, a prisoner across the range, catcalled out to him, "Hey, do us all a favor!" He slid an object from his cell to Hauffe's: a small knife—all he needed.

*Where could he have gotten that knife?* he wondered. This was a place of total confusion for Ivan Hauffe, with so many rules and just as many broken rules. He was so tired—tired and numb.

His daily anxiety attacks left him spent by nighttime. He waited until the last round for count by the guards and felt little emotion as he cut into the blankets and tore them into strips as quietly as possible. They tied together nicely; he was thankful for that.

The next morning, as dawn spread a false cloak of warmth over the institution, he was found cold, with his life choked out of him. One officer shouted for a stretcher, and another casually erased one number on the count sheet and replaced it with another.

There would be one less trip to the tower for the nation's only hangman, Radclive.

# CHAPTER 15
# INTUITION

Giselle's head ached—too many meetings, too much grief, and the constant awareness of her daughters' moods and needs. When her home was quiet, she worried about it not providing enough distraction, and when it bustled, she worried about all of them not getting enough solitude to face their emotions and sort them out in a healthy manner.

After the funeral, everyone she dealt with professionally all asked the same question, as if she had a hidden life or secret identity: why had she not given up her family name when she had married Josef? If she weren't so exhausted, she would laugh. They'd been married for ten years, and folks had waited until he was dead to ask—as if it wouldn't be proper to discuss while he was alive, as if he hadn't been aware of it.

Giselle wasn't certain she knew the answer either, as it wasn't a planned deed. It didn't occur to her until her wedding day: that leaving her family name ahead of her new married name, since it wasn't a name a child could be given as a first name to carry on a heritage, like Walter or Mason, would be personally pleasing. Boucher clearly wasn't a first name. Perhaps she knew fate would bestow only girls upon her and Josef. The banker, solicitor, and priest all asked about it. She reflected on Father Gaston's premonition the day of the funeral. He, especially, wondered about her name and whether it was telling of an "independent spirit."

Clearly he was concerned she may return to the Victorian Order of Nurses (VON) now that she was a widow, and possibly not pay full attention to her home and daughters—and perhaps not dedicate as much time to the church. She reflected on that brief time in her life before marriage, when she was a young woman venturing to remote villages and communities to provide the basic medical assistance she had trained for. She was barely in her twenties then, and it was frightening, but it softened the painful memories of her childhood, when they'd had no available medical attention for her parents and siblings. She felt purposeful. She occasionally had seen news clippings or heard of progress made by the National Council of Women and, determinedly, wanted to participate.

Spring was now summer, with rampant insect life and noises from the birds and the wind in the greenery and grass. Giselle planted a garden as usual, and the feel of earth on her hands grounded her. Her husband now lay in that ground.

How did her family get to this state? Why did that farmer come into their lives and all but destroy them? Her home still seemed like home, but the realization that her husband would never appear again gripped her. It was a cycle: the pain, and then the fear, and then the disbelief. She knew she had powerful coping skills, but she called upon her faith evening after evening, in the silence when the children were asleep and caring visitors had left. She prayed earnestly and let herself surrender to deep thought.

The news of the farmer's death at the prison was spreading around the valley, and the citizens of Loren were speculating and telling the story over and over. Each time they encountered one another, they succumbed, revisiting the details of the murder, the trial, and now the suicide of the eccentric, volatile farmer driven to the edge of his emotional capacity.

A man capable of murder and taking his own life had been living among them for a couple of years; yet he was unknown to most, as his family had kept to themselves. The townsfolk wondered about Hauffe's life before he had come from Europe to Renfrew County, and about his wife and sons, all of whom were somewhat strange and invisible. The entire family had a sickly, malnourished look about them, as though they never rested or ate properly. It was rumored that, while Hauffe was alive, the wife and sons had been treated no better than animals, with nothing but basic living conditions and subjected to hostile outbursts. Would the farm keep going without the father?

Carefully worded conversations among some of Giselle's acquaintances about the state of the farmer's sons and wife, and their finding it easy to blame Josef for the loss of their husband and father, were making the rounds. Her friends' husbands had explained to their wives, who in turn let Giselle know in the nicest possible manner, that Hauffe's instability could be a hereditary flaw in the family. The vindictive and emotional young Ivan—where was he?

When venturing out of her home, Giselle had been cautious, feeling like a spectacle, with people treating her as if she were made of glass. Her daughters never went anywhere without her now; the reality of losing their father had hurled them into a psychological space of constant fear over losing their mother and perhaps each other.

Father Gaston visited Giselle's home after church every Sunday, briefly, as he made other stops in the village and surrounding area. He tried to reach out to the other widow, too, but to no avail. Mrs. Hauffe would have no visitors, and his attempts to either talk to her on the street during a chance encounter or at her farmhouse always resulted in an aggressive interruption by young Ivan, who was impenetrable.

Worse than that were the rumors that Ivan blamed Josef for enraging his father and driving him to murdering madness. Could he possibly be seeking further revenge on Josef's innocent wife and children?

Casually the priest broached the topic with Giselle. She listened but didn't look surprised. She mentioned that this likely wasn't what the priest was referring to when he told her she would have a rough time after the burial. She added that she and her friends had discussed this topic already and let him know she was well aware of the possibility of Ivan attempting to exact revenge on the family.

Father Gaston acknowledged what Giselle said and, realizing he was speaking to an intelligent woman, decided not to patronize her. Instead he came outright with the question. "Do you fear for your physical safety? Obviously your emotional condition will be compromised for who knows how long. Have you thought about having a family member, hopefully a brother, stay with you and the girls?"

Giselle thought Luc was in the area still, as he'd said he had things to take care of there—something about drumming up some sales from local people in the county for a company he worked for. A nomad, he never stayed in one place for long. Yet she had been feeling his presence; maybe it was her fear speaking and her subconscious self-preservation taking over. She promised Father Gaston she would look into it.

As for the suicide of the farmer, her thoughts and feelings went in many directions. First, a sense of revenge filled her temporarily, and with it the sour taste of disgust for her own cruel thoughts that managed to surface before she could smother them. This was followed by her dwelling in a vast emotional expanse that was devoid of anything sensible to explain Josef's murder. Was it just a terrible misfortune? That wasn't acceptable. She deserved more. She admitted the son's hostility and possible grudge unsettled her, but going forward into the future was a must. That was her mission now.

Father Gaston wasn't without strategy or about to miss an opportunity. He cautioned her regarding her intent to take up with the VON again and assisting with medical needs in the community. He advised her that any unnecessary trips into the community would make her more vulnerable, and that until they knew more about the state of young Ivan, it would be best to remain at home until enough time had passed for the Hauffes to process their grief and anger.

Giselle stiffened "in no way does my fate have anything to do with your assessment of what is a proper for me!". What about *her* grieving period? Shouldn't she be the hostile one? She felt if she spoke bravely she might actually become that way.

# CHAPTER 16
# LIMESTONE PALACE

Father Gaston traveled to the city of Kingston with a heavy heart. He likely wouldn't attend a burial like this one again in his lifetime. He had never been in a federal prison before, even though Montreal had several. The last rites of the condemned was something he had successfully avoided.

Hauffe had been one of his flock, although he hadn't seen the man in church, and his wife had attended just once or twice. Even though she was nowhere to be found, he made this trip for her. That was partly true; he also was there because Giselle was Luc's sister. Luc didn't know the priest, but Father Gaston was no stranger to the young man's employer. He hadn't revealed to Giselle that he was aware of the relationship or what he knew about Tristan Kaye. He would keep that information to himself and reveal it to her only if necessary.

A guard admitted him through the front gate of the penitentiary, with the slamming metal resonating behind him. A group of officers walked him to the cemetery, its vastness shocking. Beside a freshly dug grave stood the warden, a psychiatric doctor, and two inmates waiting in the background to cover the coffin when summoned. The institutional chaplain approached quietly. The service was hastened, as black clouds were imminent. A hard life was ended right there in the cold ground. Where could the family be?

Other questions were circling in his mind—not lighting anywhere, just circling. The attack of Josef—there had been so much hatred. What had transpired between the two? As far as anyone knew, they were relatively unacquainted.

Father Gaston prayed silently, in French, and thought of his family and growing up in Montreal. They all had survived a house fire in the dead of winter. He had been lucky to have had gentle, loving parents, guiding him to his calling.

There had been painful moments—days and even months—in his life, but mostly it had been fulfilling. He would like to figure some things out—things about himself, not necessarily life in general—but maybe that wasn't meant to be.

There was something chilling about the burial, and he felt the need to return to the village immediately. The weather and his mood fed each other. He wanted to be home, sipping brandy in his comfortable living quarters. He was glad he had arranged for an automobile; he was a priest, not a monk.

# CHAPTER 17
# FIRST SIGHTING

Within a few hot days, a summer storm whipped up in the valley. The humidity had soared, and the hot, damp air went upward into the evening sky, bringing a torrential downpour and strong winds. Giselle stood on the second level of the house with Marie and Elise, looking through the window at their property with a hurricane lamp.

Feeling uneasy, she stayed awake long into the night, after the girls had fallen asleep. In the morning she roused herself to tend to the stabled animals. They owned just two horses, and Will helped on a regular basis, but she was working up to being able to enter the stable and shop without cringing, panicking, and reliving her memories of Josef's death.

The moment she exited the house, she stopped cold; young Ivan was in plain view. He stood on the road—not quite on her property—perfectly still, facing her, expressionless. Giselle backed slowly through the side door of her house, locked it, and raced to lock the other door. She positioned herself to cautiously look out toward the road from the kitchen window. Ivan stared motionlessly for a few minutes and then continued walking down the road toward the main part of the village. What was he doing on the low road? He lived within walking distance but not from that direction. It was obvious, Giselle thought; he was encroaching and had wanted her to see him.

She couldn't be sure he wasn't darting off into the trees to circle back and approach from a different angle. She frantically wondered how long he had been there and whether this had happened before. She couldn't take herself away from the windows in the house and wouldn't let the girls outside until she determined a plan of action.

As on the day of the funeral, Luc appeared out of nowhere. There was no response to his knock on the door, so he called out. Giselle let him in and didn't have to say much; he saw relief in her eyes and realized something had frightened her. She briefly outlined what had happened, and he listened intently. He would be in the area for a few months, he said, but hesitated to tell her why, just that his employer,

a Montreal mogul, had him working out some transporting issues in the area.

Giselle knew exactly why he was being vague, and
she sensed he was hoping she wouldn't dig too deeply. "At some point you'll explain every damn detail to
me, Luc, but fortunately for you, I have other pressing
issues right now."

After supper they sat by the fire in the front room
with Marie and Elise. Giselle was grateful her brother
was there. After she sent the girls to bed, they discussed the situation and sipped brandy to relax. Luc
thought she should consider letting him confront
young Ivan and set him straight while trying to ascertain a sense of his mood.

If mental illness were hereditary, then there may
be no end in sight to the uncertainty and unsettling
behavior. Or Giselle and the girls could relocate to
another part of the valley or to Quebec—perhaps
Montreal, where Luc spent most of his time. Their
sister, Aline, had a small family there and would wel-
come them at any time.

"At the very least, I'll leave you with a rifle or pis-
tol," Luc said. "I have several. I buy and sell them all
the time."

Giselle raised an eyebrow to this statement. Was
this how he made a living?

He continued. "I have some lightweight ones that
are easy for women to handle."

She wasn't listening or speaking until the second shot of brandy finally had relaxed her racing mind, which now wandered to more peaceful methods of resolving her angst.

Giselle now wanted to talk, with both Luc and Father Gaston, as they understood her fully, and it was one small way of assuaging her fears. She mentioned wanting to see her doctor, as perhaps he could offer some professional advice for her insomnia, which was making her anxious and testy.

Two days later the village doctor came to her home upon the priest's request. His diagnosis was more of a warning that, if Giselle didn't relax and sleep, she would be of no good to her family and would get swept into a vortex of mental fragility. Since he was her intended liaison for a possible position with the Victorian Order of Nurses, she carefully listened and held her tears in check.

He left her with a few sleeping pills, but she made a mental note not to take them in case she needed to rouse herself in the middle of the night to deal with an intruder. She didn't take well to being vulnerable; in fact it was draining her.

Luc would be around long enough to figure out what Ivan was up to. That night Giselle talked herself into a more positive mood and slept well for the first time in several weeks.

# CHAPTER 18
# THE TAKEOVER

Luc shook the hand of the tall, lean man waiting for him by the large sandbar on the Helle, just outside Loren. He was serious looking and studied Luc for a moment before stating his name, Mathew Wagoshig. He said he was from an Algonquin community nearby. He was a contact of Tristan's, and Luc was instructed to treat him well, as he had played an integral role in the overland hauls for other distributors, and Tristan was hoping for an exclusive relationship.

Mathew was respected and well connected with the best of guides, and his integrity and dedication kept him in Tristan's closest circle. The government was getting in Tristan's way with its damn treaties looming; it was a reality in the West, and he'd never heard of anything so ludicrous. He could protect Mathew to a certain extent, keep him working near his estate mostly, as he would be required to appear near there to deal with agents and authorities. The Atlantic lads weren't in on this initial meeting with Mathew, as they could be particularly undiplomatic at times.

Luc explained the plan regarding the brew that Jon Lewis made, as well as where it was and the expected level of production. It wouldn't be a large quantity, but it was of good quality, and there would be more just like him in this area who could produce. Mathew knew of bigger production caches up the Opeongo Line, but the quality lacked. If it could be blended to taste better, Tristan would consider working it into their shipments, which would require establishing a local production point.

Some of their shipments were going downriver and out to sea, but now the overland route, with men and horses to Lake Ontario, was imminent, and they would need a guide. Mathew explained where a particular north point of Lake Ontario was and the intended destination of a port near Rochester in Monroe County in the United States. "I know exactly where these locations are. It should be easy to plan the shortest route," Mathew said, unfazed. He had reliable contacts all the way to the Great Lakes, who could assist and were well experienced navigating that terrain.

"Come to my home and share a meal—we need to get to know one another." Mathew stated the plan to Luc casually, yet he had a serious demeanor about him. They were continually reading each other now.

Keeping Tristan's high regard for the man in mind, Luc realized the offer was not to be taken lightly. "I am hungry and could use a rest before returning to my sister's." He was feeling anxious to get the job started and for his newly forming relationship with Wagoshig to go well. He wondered if his own lack of knowledge of the particular route to Lake Ontario was a glaring handicap on his part. "I suspect you will have a lot to tell me about the bush—the way to the lake. I hear it is a rugged trail."

Mathew wasn't sharing any thoughts at the moment. Luc didn't doubt the man had strong opinions—he was likely investing his energy in assessing Luc's capabilities.

"I built it when my first boy came along," Mathew offered simply when they'd reached his home. The house was constructed from logs, precisely measured, cut and chinked. He had been born where the house stood but in a much cruder structure.

Luc admired without being overt. "There is a variety of wood here...unusual..."

"I wanted all logs to be the same size—didn't care what kind of tree I chopped. It only took a few days to build." Mathew looked away, nonchalantly.

At first Luc's brow puckered slightly in disbelief and then relaxed as Mathew continued. "I had a lot of help," Mathew grinned, delighting in the small joke. "If people don't help each other with things that are difficult, how can anything get accomplished?"

Was this his way of telling Luc he wasn't going to hold his lack of experience with backwoods trekking against him?

Mathew took care of the unspoken question. "There will be times when you would swear we are traveling in circles or that east is west and north is south. If you give in to what your thoughts lead you to and leave me, you will probably die of exposure. It's up to you."

"I have no intention of leaving you. We will both be well paid—it has to be successful. And the only way it can is if we stay together." Luc was caught off guard with the change in tone and quickly reverted back to business talk—his new friend seemed to favor mixing it in with personal conversation randomly.

"OK, let me show you around my place." Mathew continued the tour.

The property was well defined with a log fence, securing the family of five and keeping Mathew's three young sons safe from curious childhood adventures to nearby Muskrat Lake, one of the largest cold lakes for miles.

"The kids around here like to play games by the lake and even on it in the winter...seeing if the ice will hold when they all gather on a spot. It usually doesn't."

"I grew up on the St. Lawrence—winter games are the hardest to resist," Luc said and nodded.

A striking young woman appeared in the doorway, smiling and inviting Luc inside.

They shared a meal in the quiet company of Mathew's family and then sipped rose-hip tea as they discussed business. Mathew listened to the story of the murder of Luc's brother-in-law and the disturbing sighting of young Ivan and commented, simply, that it seemed to him the farmer and his son must be ill-tempered. Perhaps, he suggested, the ways of this country differed so from their origins that they couldn't contain their frustration. He offered that there was no explaining some things, and perhaps the situation should be taken care of soon.

Luc conceded his concern. "My good man," he said, "I think of little else at the moment."

The next day they met again, scoping out the trek to Jon Lewis's place, and discussed what the rest of the journey would entail by corroborating what they both knew to be true. Mathew had worked this particular trail previously and knew it well.

He explained the importance of preparing for the possible challenges of traversing the sloped shale in wet weather and crossing the heavier streams. He and Luc would be overseeing the collection of several caches of alcohol from different brewers located in the valley and toward the north point of Lake Ontario, where it would be stashed and loaded onto a laker as quickly as possible to head for a port near Rochester. Getting the liquid into kegs would require some planning; some of it would be picked up that way, while other brewers provided their brew only in bottles and jugs.

A great deal of hard work, trekking, and reporting had taken place over the past year, and Luc knew this particular venture was his chance to carve himself an earned spot in the hierarchy of Tristan Kaye's esteemed organization. He was long past being new and inexperienced and took pride in his organizational skills and his talent for bringing out the best in his men while keeping their respect.

He imagined himself buying a luxurious home in Montreal on the hill, owning a fleet of automobiles, and living a full life. He didn't eschew progress like his late brother-in-law, and nothing could impede him now.

That night Luc stayed for another meal at the Wagoshigs' home; the two had bonded quickly, as predicted by Tristan. He then hastily rode back to Giselle and his nieces to find them safe, with nothing further to report.

Luc would see Jon Lewis the following week to ensure that the pickup he and Mathew would make would be ready, and Tristan would arrange for his men to meet with other similarly arranged loads. If the plan were successful, at least ten other groups would converge, and then the whole entourage, led by Mathew, would head to Lake Ontario. Luc and Mathew would kick off the mission together; the plan was as smooth as a mirror. Luc had a week to organize and lie low, maybe even relax.

The next morning he asked Giselle if she needed anything done around the property; they still hadn't decided what to do about Josef's business and tools. She wasn't ready to sell them off and didn't need to, so they stayed where they were for the time being. She became visibly upset just by talking about the shop and Josef's things. Her demeanor changed quickly these days; she looked thin, too.

Malcolm Rast and Stuart Sheen would be appearing that night and staying at the Loren Village Hotel. At dusk Luc walked to the village's main street. He could appreciate his sister's fondness for this place.

He hesitated and then entered the hotel's tavern, thinking the Atlantic lads might be there.

He was right, and once inside he stopped short unexpectedly, stood tall, and greeted a stranger to the village, a man flanked by Rast, Sheen, and a few other familiar faces. Tristan Kaye shook Luc's hand, leaned into him, and said he thought he would make a few exploratory trips, and that this village was central to several of his new intended suppliers of spirits.

Tristan was impeccably dressed and looked somewhat out of place. Luc smiled as he admired the man and felt the more time he spent with him, the more he could learn. Tristan would leave in the morning on his own journey, via actual roads, to the destination port on Lake Ontario, where eventually as many of the bottles as possible would be kegged and loaded onto a laker. He then would take a private boat across the lake to meet with Tom Carter in Rochester.

Luc was invited to sit and talk with Tristan; the others were not, as their roles were more security oriented while they accompanied him on business trips. Not that long ago, that had been Luc's duty too, but Tristan had identified him as a clever, diplomatic, and persuasive type and had promoted him to organizer fairly quickly.

They chatted in a more casual manner, and the topic of the death of Luc's brother-in-law arose. Luc had loved, admired, and respected Josef as a businessman in a dying craft, passed on by his ancestors. His concern for his sister and nieces showed.

Speaking from experience, Tristan advised Luc about things he may never have thought of regarding the state of a person who has lost a spouse. "A woman doesn't have the same opportunities to vent pent-up frustration that a man does—to drink or fight to subdue the storm in her soul," he said. "When I lost Madeline, my mind went to places I hadn't known before."

Luc hadn't known much about Tristan's personal life and worked the opportunity; it never hurt to get closer to the boss.

At ten o'clock Tristan retired to his hotel room, and Luc proceeded to Giselle's house. The walk was pleasant, and the air gentle in the summer ambience. The words of his unexpected companion for the evening lingered in his thoughts.

The next morning Giselle, the girls, and Luc made their way to church. Father Gaston was in fine form for Mass. He hadn't seen Luc since the funeral and of course was pleased he'd been staying with Giselle.

Unexpectedly, once again, Tristan appeared, seated in the back pew. Luc remembered something about his attending Mass every Sunday, and while it had been unplanned, he felt it was providential that he had decided to attend with Giselle.

Afterward he introduced Tristan to his sister and nieces. Tristan was gracious and conversed briefly about their village. Giselle was relieved to see an associate of Luc's who appeared to be civilized and of substance. Perhaps his life wasn't as shady as she had come to suspect.

To everyone's disbelief, Father Gaston, caught off guard, greeted Tristan warmly, as they previously had been acquainted in a church community in Montreal. Giselle's interest was piqued, as it was somewhat unbelievable that her brother and Father Gaston could have a common connection. Her curiosity got the best of her, and in an impulsive moment, she invited Tristan to join them at her home for a midday meal. Perhaps she could find out more information about Luc's work this way and avoid a head-on interrogation, which he likely would charm his way out of.

Tristan hesitated but then agreed. Although he was on a scheduled journey, he said a delay of a few hours wouldn't matter. He would need to speak to some of his men first, and then he would join them.

*What an interesting day*, Luc mused. He was about to sit down to a meal with Tristan Kaye—and in his sister's home even. The Atlantic boys would be envious.

Once at home, Giselle busied herself with the meal, her thoughts turning to Josef and how much he enjoyed Sunday dinners. She'd need to deal with the shop and tools soon; he had no siblings, and his parents were long deceased.

Her thoughts were interrupted by the presence of Luc, who looked puzzled and concerned. He told her he had been in the shop, where he discovered the tongs, back in the spot where Josef had kept them. This made no sense, as the police had taken them as evidence.

In the recent past, Luc and Giselle had discussed the empty hooks and their shadow on the wall; their conspicuous absence had been a constant reminder. Could this be a different set of tongs? Could young Ivan have placed them there as some kind of threat? She didn't want to see them, different or not. Luc went back into the shop and stable to take a hard look around. He made a mental note to take his own advice and make good on a rifle for himself and Giselle.

The arrival of Tristan distracted the pair, and the good meal, stimulating conversation, and brandy in the middle of the day alleviated the mysterious mood. Luc again related his concern regarding young Ivan's hostility, his strange appearance on the road, and even the priest's concern.

Tristan listened and addressed Giselle in a sage manner. "Mrs. Reicher, I suggest you contact the authorities and make a report." Before he could elaborate further, a knock on the door broke the weighty atmosphere. It was a casual, friendly knock; Will wanted to check on the horses and the family. Giselle invited him in to meet Tristan and join the others.

It occurred to Luc that Will was in and out of the buildings frequently, and perhaps he had something to do with the tongs reappearing. Curious, he stood and asked him directly.

Will looked affronted and then asked Luc to sit down, as he had something to tell them about—the conversation between young Ivan and his father while he was locked in the holding cell. He had no idea how far the insult to the family pride would go. Even worse, the village was buzzing about how there was no sign of Mrs. Hauffe anywhere. In the past she had ventured to the village and market at least once a week, and Father Gaston had tried one last time to visit her, only to have young Ivan tell him she had left with her most precious belongings. The young man didn't seem overly concerned and refused to answer any further questions.

Giselle indicated she would have liked to have known this earlier but could see Will had struggled with making her feel more upset at a vulnerable time. The two visitors realized she needed to digest all that had transpired and said their good-byes to their gracious hostess. Finding himself in unknown territory with his sister, Luc stoked the fire and sat quietly.

He was accustomed to living a life of uncertainty at times, but couldn't fathom how his sister was living that life now too. He had an uneasy feeling about it.

One thing Giselle made up her mind about was an opportunity Father Gaston had presented. He was about to embark upon a trip to Montreal and offered to take her daughters to her sister's house; it would be good to give the girls a break from what was going on at home. Giselle discussed the idea with Elise and Marie, and there was no persuasion required. A trip to Montreal to Aline's was arranged, with hasty packing and excitedly made plans. It was very good timing.

The next morning Luc prepared for his trip with Mathew Wagoshig. With new takeovers, there was always an initial trip or two in order to learn as much as possible "from the ground up," as Tristan preached.

Luc's ability to read people, persuade them, and motivate them hadn't gone unnoticed by his boss, and he was assigned to oversee the shipments down the St. Lawrence to Halifax as well as distribution there. It was a big job, as there were always opportunities to sell off the cargo in Halifax for a very decent profit, but that would leave the Americans without as much as anticipated. It wasn't a good idea, but the demand in Nova Scotia was just as great, especially for plain, crude, high-test brew. They called it "Everclear," "Pure

Test," and other vague names, and it could mean a death sentence if one drank it like rum.

It was always tempting to set some of the cargo aside and sell for a high price on the short-term request in Halifax. The city was thirsty. But Luc hadn't given in yet and didn't plan to. Tristan wouldn't put up with that.

Luc proceeded to the stable to check the cart and horses. He shivered when he was within one hundred feet of the building. Maybe his sister should think about relocating; the girls would love Montreal, and Aline was desperate to see her sister and nieces.

# CHAPTER 19
# THE CALM

Summoning all her courage, Giselle focused on the matters at hand. The shop and stable, for instance, required attention, especially as the tools and equipment were valuable. Luc's supply of whiskey was a godsend. It was pleasant, warm, and slowed her racing pulse every time, without fail. She'd never taken even a sip of whiskey while Josef was alive, which made her laugh. It also was proving easier sorting things out without the children around.

She tried to take on a businesslike persona, at least for a short time. She had strength and good sense. She would auction off the valuables; she didn't want to see them anymore. Josef wouldn't want her reminded constantly anyway. He was with her but in small, surprising ways, nothing conspicuous—just subtle encounters. He had been a modest, conservative man, and being overt wasn't his style.

She found the iron gate he had forged and instantly knew it was for her. Seeing it took her breath away, and she walked away from it, out to the road, which was lined with firs and cedars. Suddenly she felt incensed—why shouldn't she feel comfortable taking a walk on her own property? She left her fear and discomfort behind and walked calmly down the road, admiring the beauty of the valley forest and looking toward the Helle. She heard waterfowl on the river, even though they weren't in view.

Giselle walked a brave mile, until she came to the railway tracks, and then she began the reverse journey home. All that was missing was Josef; this was their stroll. There was a small hidden lake nearby, and loons called their haunting whistles. She realized this was the first time since the funeral she had felt at peace. There would be absolutely no letting go of it now.

# CHAPTER 20
# PREPARATION

L uc kept himself distracted with work. He had co-ordination issues to sort out. All the cargo was to be gathered at the large sandbar over the next few days and would be well hidden of course. Horses had to be readied, and carts and wagons needed to be inspected. He worked closely with Mathew Wagoshig, who remained unnervingly calm and steady at all times; obviously he was a seasoned guide. They had arranged an impressive convoy, and Luc hoped the roads and trails wouldn't prove troublesome. He had hired two men to handle wagon and cart repairs, should there be a breakdown. He almost made an of-fer to Will Frank, as he was a horseman of sorts, but thought he might not be interested in carrying illegal cargo. Maybe next time he would inquire. Besides,

Will was reliably looking in on Giselle and the property, which was paramount.

Weapons were checked and inventoried but likely would be used only for shooting game to eat along the way. Luc recently had acquired a Colt .455 and liked it so much that he had picked up a second one. He would choose a small rifle or maybe a shotgun to leave with Giselle.

After cleaning the stable one evening, Will had shown her how to operate his shotgun. She didn't like it but seemed to catch on. She'd had a new demeanor over the past few days—more peaceful and steady as she went about her affairs. She no longer appeared to be constantly trying to figure out why and how things had evolved and seemed to be making the best of her life.

Hopefully Rast and Sheen were at the top of Lake Ontario, waiting for Tristan, who purportedly was journeying on to see Tom Carter. Carter likely would buy everything they had. Rast and Sheen wouldn't be holding the money; they hadn't been promoted to that rank yet, but if they gained Tristan's trust over time, they too could earn more status by protecting the financial men who worked for Tristan—delivering them and the cash to the bank.

# CHAPTER 21
# CULMINATION OF PERIL

The solicitor had processed Josef's will, and the deposit had been made to the family's bank account. Now Giselle had to have the business account and joint account put in her name only. She hadn't had frequent dealings with the banker, and when she had, it always had been with Josef, so she welcomed Luc's presence on this mission.

Luc and Giselle made their way into Loren together, wanting to appear oblivious to the curious public. The townspeople looked at them inquisitively but then glanced away quickly to ensure they wouldn't engage in conversation, as the awkwardness of asking a woman how she was coping with a murder in her family was unthinkable. They didn't know how to look at people who'd experienced tragedy, let alone talk to them.

Giselle used the emotional space afforded her by her community to her advantage. She didn't want to delve into the mystery anymore; it was time to move on. The heavy lilac sweetness in the summer air helped keep her buoyant and steady. At least she convinced herself that was the case.

The thoughts and concerns of the brother and sister grew so loud that the idea of not speaking openly was now ludicrous. Maybe this leisurely stroll together was an opportunity to be honest with each other.

Luc dove right in. "Are you letting the rumors get to you?"

"I'm more than concerned," Giselle told him. "I've been burying the possibility of being harmed, but when I ask myself if I want to bring the girls home, the answer is a definite no. That confirms what I'm feeling, even if I don't admit it." She looked to her brother for feedback.

"Did you know the mother and younger brother haven't been seen anywhere, and young Ivan appears to be at the farm alone? No one's been brave enough to challenge him regarding whether he's contacted the authorities. He told some folks that his mother went on a trip with his brother. I find that unsettling."

"You're debating whether to go on your business trip, aren't you?" Giselle said. "You must go. I can see you have a great opportunity, although the details aren't completely clear to me. Your boss seems to be a respectable character as well. You can't stay for me, Luc. If I become too fearful, I'll get some friends to stay with me." She was firm on that topic.

"Friends?" he retorted. "Do you think your lady friends, who have families with children, would want to come out to your property where your husband was taken without good reason? I know you'd do it for any of them, as you're an independent soul, but it's not likely to be the sentiment of the town. Yes, I'm struggling with this deeply."

Giselle placed a hand on her brother's shoulder. "It may not look right, but I could ask Will to stay in the loft in the shop." She shook her head. "No, he's probably too fearful to do that, and I can't invite him into the house, as ridiculous as that is." Giselle was determined to find a solution. They were now in front of the bank and entered. "Let's just get this over with and then get me up to speed with the shotgun." She laughed at Luc's surprised expression.

The business was taken care of, by Giselle, in a competent manner, leaving Luc more time to ponder his dilemma while the brisk conversation about interest rates, where to sign, and fine print droned in the background. They departed, linked arms, and started the long walk home.

A familiar, sleek, healthy-looking horse was tethered to a post at the edge of the village where they approached the low road. Mathew Wagoshig greeted them, and it was evident he urgently needed to speak with Luc.

Luc requested that he walk back to the house with them and join them for a meal while they talked. Mathew agreed and, careful about discussing business in front of Giselle, kept the conversation light. The three discussed the growing season, as was common for townspeople making small talk. Giselle recalled how Josef had gotten exasperated with that conversation with local farmers, and he'd always raised a flag against suggestions of farming; he wouldn't want to depend upon the weather.

Luc sensed her thoughts and said it for her. "Josef would love this conversation." This moment of sharing made them all laugh.

Temporarily lighthearted, they approached the yard, all three knowing that while Giselle prepared a meal, Mathew and Luc would go outside to discuss business. She hoped they wouldn't; she was certainly mature and intelligent enough to engage in their conversation, but that's how things were, and she inwardly promised to do all she could to effect change in the world regarding such things.

She observed them chatting casually outside, smoking and gesturing, the fullness of late summer all around them. It was almost time to harvest what she had planted. Luc was pointing toward the house vaguely; she knew he was talking about her. He rubbed his face with his hands, as if washing it with what was likely an attempt to clear his mind. If he were wrestling with guilt, she wouldn't be able to hold herself back from going out there and sorting out their dilemma, whatever it was. He had to take the journey he had planned to take.

The two men returned to the house, but only Luc entered the kitchen to speak with her.

"Mathew and I have an issue to take care of about twenty miles away," he told Giselle. "I can't explain, but I'm going with him for a couple of days. If things go all right for you while I'm gone, I'll make the longer trip for the job. Father Gaston and Will can check on you. All right?" He wasn't wavering but politely asking whether she was comfortable.

Giselle agreed to the arrangement and resisted further discussion, as she knew he was sick about leaving her. But life had to resume; she frequently felt numb, but that was better than fear and pain. Her plans to ready herself to work again were her rock.

After supper Luc and Mathew departed. Traveling in the darkness? She hadn't been able to get out of them what they were tending to—something about a shipment they were coordinating for Tristan. Restaurant supplies eventually would be transported to Rochester. She knew Tristan was in the restaurant business, and it was far-reaching. He had come from Ireland originally and chosen not to carry on the family shipbuilding business on the Canadian coast. He preferred Montreal and must have done well, as Luc had described his massive wealth.

Still, it seemed odd that restaurant supplies couldn't be obtained locally in Rochester. She would have that awaited talk with Luc in the near future and get more details.

The evening was perfectly serene. Giselle admired the way Mathew and Luc had left evidence in the yard to make it appear she wasn't alone. A few pairs of boots were on the doorstep and a light was burning in the loft of the shop. Two extra sacks of horse feed stood near the stable, even though it was locked, with no extra livestock inside.

She had brought back fashion catalogs from the village and paged through them, attempting to rekindle her interest in fine clothes and accessories. The reading was so light that she was sleepy in a reasonable time, without taking a sleeping pill either. She rested comfortably in the middle of her bed. Most of the night was good to her; the tossing started close to morning, as usual. Her mind was overstimulated, and she occasionally experienced near panic about being alone in the world without her husband. Daytime wasn't a problem—just those damn predawn hours.

She roused herself very early and brewed some tea. After dressing, she prepared to sit quietly in the kitchen and write in her journal. Then she'd prepare her letter to the Victorian Order of Nurses about re-instatement. She had given this careful consideration and felt empowered and fortunate that, all strife aside, she might be given the opportunity to work again. The day flew by as Giselle carefully penned a final draft of an eloquent three-page proposal to the VON.

Startled by Will's knock at her door, she greeted him, unaware it was nearly suppertime. It had been a day all to herself and well spent. Will had come by, as he'd promised Luc, to confirm she was safe and un-disturbed. After a brief conversation and an inspec-tion of the yard and shop, Will went home to tend to his father.

Giselle was hungry and thirsty; for several hours she'd done nothing but focus on composing the let-ter. She made a light supper and prepared the letter for posting tomorrow.

While pouring the steaming dishwater into the sink, she suddenly grew chilly. She performed a slow, deliberate about-face to determine, warily, the cause of the chilly feeling. The front door was ajar.

The air wasn't particularly cool, making her aware that something other than the evening atmosphere was making her uneasy. She knew Will had closed the door when he had left; in her haste to prepare her meal, she must not have secured the lock. She had to approach the door in order to close and lock it, but she sensed someone was on the other side of it.

Could she be experiencing some paranoia that might have been subconsciously suppressed? Giselle forced herself to reach for the door handle. As swiftly as possible, she lunged at the door, slammed it, and locked it.

The sound of the door coincided with the shattering of the kitchen window. Recoiling, she went to the front window, where she saw the figure she'd never wanted to see again. Wearing a strangely heavy coat and looking gaunt, he hadn't seen her shadow in the front window yet.

His eyes searched the front of the house, as if expecting her to appear in the form of vapor from a crack somewhere. He yelled as if addressing fifty or more, an imagined audience that filled the entire house and yard. "I promised I would send you and the liar to your graves! I promised my father. You'll both see him on the other side!"

Giselle remained silent, stunned by what was behind young Ivan, undetected by him. An automobile passing on the low road to the village backfired, causing the young man to startle and dash into the bushes in the yard. As he was now completely out of view, she was at a disadvantage. Where was the shotgun? A few steps away in a cabinet in the dining room. She needed to grab it and shift her focus back outside before he moved. She could outwait him; the way she felt now, she never would stop waiting.

Two hours passed. She had been gripping the shotgun in the darkness, and finally she spied movement farther away than where he had disappeared. Then...nothing. All her senses were heightened, and what normally would go undetected was very audible. Giselle heard footsteps crunching on the gravel around the side of the house, approaching the front door, hesitating, and then walking back several paces. Would he break down the door? She wondered whether he had a rifle or handgun she hadn't seen. She saw him move around the side of the house, approaching a window. Thank God she had closed the shutters.

As she crept upstairs in the darkness, she wondered whether her daughters believed in her ability to protect them. They weren't here, but she wouldn't put up with this intimidation tactic any longer. From the bedroom she easily could see down the stairs to the more well-lit main floor and also out the window. She positioned herself to the side of the bedroom window; the moonlight illuminated the outdoors and made it much brighter out there—perfect. Ivan wouldn't be able to see inside.

He moved in a sideways manner into full view and stood thirty feet from the front door. He stood still and then reached into his coat and brandished something shiny. Was it a gun, a knife, or some sort of bludgeoning weapon? She couldn't tell. It didn't matter; this was over for her. She cocked the hammer on the twelve-gauge shotgun. *Good decision to use it instead of a rifle,* she thought. There would be less chance of missing her target.

She discharged the weapon through her bedroom window and watched him drop—the son of Ivan Hauffe. Overcome with the situation, she buckled too, but managed to carefully set the weapon aside, never wanting to touch it again. Several images flashed in her mind simultaneously. She saw Josef looking peaceful. She saw the farmer, dead in his prison cell; she fully realized now how he had gotten to that place. Finally, she saw the image of herself as if she were outside her body, squeezing the trigger in slow motion. She remained in the upstairs of her home, huddled for several hours, until Luc returned to the house.

Giselle had passed out and then awoke from being shaken by her brother, who, after determining she was reasonably all right, told her to stay where she was. He dragged young Ivan's body into the stable and returned to her side to see whether she could speak. She was amazingly clearheaded and lucidly revealed the chain of events.

Luc was as rigid as stone, upset with himself for having left his sister. *He must have seen us leave,* he thought. They focused on trying to figure out whether they should contact the authorities or simply get rid of him. It was a long day for Luc and Giselle; the resulting plan was to dispose of young Ivan's body where it never would be found. He and Mathew were taking a cart to Jon Lewis's place to pick up the brew. They could use it and detour to one of the boggy areas where anything heavy sunk almost immediately. Rast and Sheen were miles away up the Helle with another brew maker. That decided it for Luc.

The plan was to go in the morning, as soon as Mathew arrived. Luc could count on him to keep quiet, he surmised, but would Giselle survive this?

For the next twenty-four hours, Luc's adrenaline kept him buoyant and tireless. He remained calm, steadied his sister, and insisted she stay at home and in her bed until he returned. She should have been in shock yet appeared to be fine. She claimed she was relieved and spoke of bringing her daughters home from Montreal. While her conversational skills seemed normal, he didn't want to leave her; he didn't have any idea what a true sign of her being able to cope might be. Then there were his racing thoughts about his trip. He had to decide whether his sister's plight outweighed his dream of successfully proving himself in the smuggling business and setting the stage for making more wealth than he could imagine. All of this was so ill timed. He gazed out Giselle's bedroom window as far into the distance as possible, as though the horizon might show him a sign.

# CHAPTER 22
# DELIVERY

Mathew and Luc rode in silence. The Algonquin man was as calm as Giselle had been when Luc had left her. It wasn't difficult bringing the guide on board with the plan. It was obvious he was keen and wanted the task to be a success as much as Luc did. Luc took care of the physical wrapping and loading of the corpse. He made a mental note that if he needed assistance with hiding a body in the future, he would call upon Giselle and Mathew, as calm as they were. He needed to bring some private amusement into this ride but was hardly successful.

He had seen a few deaths and subsequent cover-ups in his young life, but those were different scenes altogether—places and times where all the players knew the risks and rules. This was something else: his dear sister's limits for psychological torment.

Apparently she'd been seriously affected by Josef's murder and the looming hostility of young Ivan in ways he couldn't imagine. Clearly there was no need for him to have worried about her becoming a shrinking violet and suppressing her emotions. Luc almost couldn't endure his own thoughts at the moment.

Mathew finally spoke to indicate the slight detour off the rough trail to the required location, which was fairly close to the trail. Insects buzzed lazily in the heat in the dense brush, and the definition of the bog area was difficult to assess. Luc would have preferred a location farther from Jon Lewis's home, but his companion believed this was the softest ground and where the body would sink the quickest. They dragged the lifeless form of young Ivan, wrapped in a horse blanket, to a boggy spot and placed some heavy rocks on top of it. Luc was looking around for easily moveable brush for concealment, but Mathew abruptly said they should stop and walk back out. The rocks would do the work, and the less they disturbed the area, the better.

"Two days from now, it'll be gone," the guide reassured the young man after the brisk walk back to the trail. Luc noticed his new friend looking around casually prior to their resuming their trek to Lewis's place.

With the task completed, a more relaxed Luc let his thoughts meander to his sister's state of mind. Tristan was right; she hadn't had the opportunity to vent her angst and fears, and it had led straight to corrective action. He had no idea she was capable of taking this matter into her own hands.

# CHAPTER 23

# PURIFICATION

Mathew and Luc bedded down in a beckoning spot before proceeding to Lewis's. It wouldn't be difficult to get there that day, but they needed to rest and collect their thoughts regarding their grisly detour. The darkness was comforting, and they sat fireside in silence. Along with everything else, Luc was concerned about Mathew's state of mind. In the hypnotic, dancing light, he gave serious consideration to the situation and would choose his words carefully. At the outset Mathew had been stoic about participating in the burial of young Ivan; his attitude was one of intent focus on the main objective at hand: gathering and delivering the alcohol to the destination. His body language was tighter now, well controlled, but the slight tenseness was noticeable. The initial news of Giselle's ordeal had rendered Mathew to quiet contemplation for a few minutes after listening to the plan; then he had nodded in agreement but let Luc deal with the physical preparation.

Now, as Luc prepared to ask Mathew if he wanted to know anything further, the guide broke the silence and asked how well Giselle and Josef had known young Ivan and his father. Luc shook his head and said they'd barely known them, only by sight and from a few local stories. Mathew seemed more alert and asked about the trial and more details about Ivan Hauffe's behavior. As Luc described how the judge had ordered a mental-health assessment, Mathew became rigid. He reached into his pocket for some dried cedar, tossed it into the fire, and prayed quietly. The dry cedar was like kerosene on the flames, and Mathew deeply inhaled the smoke. Luc waited, unmoving and observing. He wanted to respect the man's rituals but also wondered why he was doing this now. Was it a regular occurrence, or had their experience caused him to want to communicate with the Creator?

Mathew finally rose and asked Luc if he wanted more tea. He seemed to be more like his usual self. After he prepared more of the hot brew for them, he crouched down with a cup in hand and casually gazed into the flames and sparks. He said only one more thing to Luc before retiring to his camp bed. "We need to purify ourselves."

That was an interesting proposition. Startled somewhat, Luc didn't respond, as he wasn't certain what was appropriate or even what the man was referring to exactly. He had heard ghastly tales of purification performed by the Iroquois in years past. These rituals involved the most severe forms of torture, sometimes self-inflicted, to ensure the soul went to the Creator in a cleansed state after death and to honor their enemy's power and their own. Mathew wasn't Iroquois or living in the old days. Why hadn't he said more? Luc knew better than to pummel him with questions, and the respect he had for the man grew daily, so he decidedly refused to tamper with that.

Feeling somewhat nauseated, Luc tossed in his camp bed, unable to warm himself. There was no real chill in the air; it was in his soul. He relived the surrealism of the inert body being rolled into the bog, the look in his sister's eyes before he'd left Loren, and the burial of another body—that of his brother-in-law Josef. Usually he drifted off to sleep comfortably, in deep thought about assessing his position within Tristan's empire, dreaming of future goals and jobs. He was living his young life to the fullest and looked forward to each new day. This night, however, was different. It held his almost lifeless, fatigued body motionless and his brain weirdly alert, horribly over-stimulated yet slipping helplessly. Strangely combined images and visions of his life passed through his mind until he slipped out of a conscious state.

Luc's mind raced from the deepest sleep as quickly as it had surrendered. He awoke early, just at dawn. His horse stood over him, its wet nose nuzzling his torso and head. Luc panicked and jumped to his feet. His head hurt, and there was a deafening noise that made it worse. The horse was obviously untied. Mathew, the cart, and his horse were nowhere to be seen. In fact nothing looked familiar—where was he? They had camped in a low spot among fir trees and quiet; he was now on a rocky slope near rushing water, alone.

Luc headed for the stream, which was tumbling over the slope; his thirst was extreme. He led the horse, as he wasn't feeling steady enough to mount it. He felt as if he had consumed a pint of whiskey the previous night, but he knew that hadn't happened. He sat on a mossy boulder with his head in his hands. Nothing made sense. Could Mathew have wanted out of the trip? If he had wanted out of the deal, he likely would have just stated his case and departed. Trying to figure out where Lewis's shack was seemed impossible. He'd been there a couple of times, but he saw none of the familiar landmarks. He needed the cart to haul the alcohol to the gathering spot—how could he get this journey back on course? If he couldn't find Mathew or his way to Lewis's, he would have no future with Tristan's league. He'd been left with nothing—no supplies, weapons, or food. He slid off the boulder and sat on the ground.

All the noises seemed exceptionally piercing. His senses were heightened, and the sunlight was blazing in the morning sky. His horse drank and grazed. Luc knew he couldn't have been more than a few hours off course or from the direction in which they had come, as Mathew couldn't have traveled very quickly at night if he had relocated Luc himself. Perhaps Mathew had been taken as well and was in peril somewhere. Struggling to make sense of his surroundings, he knew a plan was crucial. After some time, he decided to travel to a slightly higher altitude for a few hours to see if he could get his bearings from a better vantage. He would follow the stream upward and keep close to the water supply. He had awoken on bare ground with no blankets, so if it got chilly or insects thronged, he might have a problem. But the sun was high now, and the fresh magnificence that surrounded him now was his nemesis. Could he survive in it?

Luc's first objective was to determine where he was and how to get to Lewis's and then find a way to keep the job going. He was determined to deliver the brew and not let Tristan down. The second task was to figure out what had happened to Mathew and the cart. If the guide had intentionally abandoned and duped him, he could regroup and still meet his deadline. If outside forces had separated him from Mathew, and the guide was harmed or dead, the delay would be longer, and he would need to get to Tristan as soon as possible.

Luc led the horse up the slope. They both had good energy at the moment; he was thinking of what he would eat later. Spruce needles and berries could make a hot tea if he made a fire and could heat it in something, but he might be able to drink only from the stream.

Frogs and small fish would be readily available for cooking on a stick; there were some dry twigs and moss to be found. Making a fire wouldn't be an issue once he stopped and settled. There also were bitter gooseberries and a few small wild strawberries for the taking. He wasn't considering small game, as he didn't have a gun and couldn't be more than a half day's journey from home or Lewis's place. He tried not to think about his missing weapons; he really didn't believe Mathew would leave him this way intentionally. He couldn't let the mystery frustrate him and drain him of precious energy.

As dusk approached, Luc realized that while he was warm now, he might not be later, so he set off to gather what he needed to make a small fire. A half hour later, he had made a small, low shelter of cedar bows under some dense brush for when the time came to bed down. He didn't like the thunderhead clouds developing, though it was no surprise—the day was humid. He consumed the berries he had picked but didn't really need the fire that was burning, as he had no meat to cook or anything to heat water in. The rain started softly, almost a mist as it evaporated on the hot slope. Luc slid under his well-built shelter and waited it out. Hours of deafening, cracking thunder and intermittent showers lasted throughout the night, leaving him exhausted the following morning.

He was hungry, tired, and also angry and bewildered. The water hadn't seeped into his shelter, but if the storm had lasted another hour, he would have had to stand up and relocate in the wet blackness. His body ached with stiffness as the morning sun rose on the other side of the slope. He needed to get moving. The horse was fine, grazing lazily. His head ached, as he usually had a few cups of black tea or coffee in the morning. The sun didn't look as if it would break through the cloud cover, and his clothes were damp. He shivered and felt lightheaded.

How could he have ended up like this so close to home? It wasn't home, though. He knew his way around Montreal and down the river to the various villages, but this land wasn't his, and he'd been out and around in his sister's village only a few times. He needed to identify something to take him back there or to Lewis's. A wind was picking up, and no sun broke the clouds; it would be another day of bad weather. He stopped to gather some fire starter and break some more boughs. Everything was damp, though. He needed to rest and really wanted a hot cup of coffee or tea and some sleep. He sat down and leaned against a lone oak. The firs and cedars weren't comfortable to be under because of the needles. Although he didn't intend to, he drifted off to sleep as soon as he was still.

# CHAPTER 24
# MATHEW

O nly a few miles away, a determined spirit led his horse, which pulled a cart with blankets, supplies, weapons, and other cargo. They weren't on a proper road but were navigating the landscape as best they could, with the man leading the horse and not wishing to encounter any other humans.

The man was hungry, but didn't eat the provisions he had with him. He was tired, but didn't mount the horse and walked on. He sang and hummed quietly to himself at times, steady in his journey. It was a private journey for him alone to pass through. He stopped at the perfect spot—a small clearing on high ground— where he searched for the best logs and felled wood. The construction took most of the day, and he had to stop and rest frequently, as he had consumed only water for the past couple of days. He worked hard and slow, locating and entwining poles with just the right forks at their ends. The structure had to be eight feet by three feet and as high as he could make it. The only consideration for height was how much wood he could place underneath it. The platform had to support a couple of hundred pounds.

He finished and stopped to burn some tobacco and pray. He prayed quietly, sometimes getting louder, until he had barely any voice. That was the sign. He stopped and lay down to rest on the bare ground with no cover. He was waiting for the panic-filled hallucinations and mental terror. His ancestors would be speaking to him, guiding him through the journey. He had heard stories of others' experiences, and he knew that once the fear and discomfort passed, he would sleep. Then, when he woke up, he would begin the work. The Creator would wake him at the right time.

# CHAPTER 25
# LUC

L uc awoke to insects swarming around his ravaged skin, thirsty for more blood. He wobbled over to the stream for a drink, his head aching and stomach growling. He had kept some twigs and moss in his shirt and made a small fire, after which he forced himself to search for kindling and larger pieces of wood to burn. His head finally cleared a little. He would have to think of a way to snare larger game to eat. But first he had to remember what the landscape looked like on his previous trip to Lewis's and perhaps climb a tree to scan the bush.

For the first time in two days, he wondered about Giselle. He'd been extremely focused on this job, but Giselle needed him. That was another reason he needed to get back on track and on the trail. He coughed, breathing the smoke from his fire. Then the cold realization washed over him—his fire was down-wind, and he was breathing a heavier smoke from the other direction. This could be good if it meant help was near. Or it could be a sweeping forest fire started by the thunderstorm.

Luc stamped out his fire, grabbed the horse's reigns, and headed in the direction of the smoke. It was a calculated risk, but he saw the smoke was on the nearby horizon, stemming from one spot and not in a wide swathe. He was relieved, but realized he had to approach cautiously, as he was unarmed and not feel-ing strong should an unfriendly encounter ensue—if he did in fact find people or a person at the fire.

As he walked the smell changed, faintly resem-bling cooked meat and plain woodsmoke, but there was a stench along with it that played with his senses and made his empty stomach clench and heave. His horse gently resisted heading toward the source of smoke, so he changed direction slightly to approach it from the side. Then he saw Mathew, sitting and praying quietly with his eyes closed, beside a roaring fire created underneath what was left of a body on a platform.

The end of something that Luc recognized was burning or melting, fluttering in the waves of the heat. It was the blanket in which they had wrapped young Ivan's body. Not far away were the cart, along with the supplies and weapons.

Luc couldn't make sense of the scene. He called to Mathew, who stood and put his hands up for Luc to stop walking. Was he going to get a weapon in order to finish him off and burn him too? Luc stopped. They both were still until the guide asked Luc if he understood what was happening. Luc resisted getting angry, mostly because he felt weak. Mathew stated calmly that they wouldn't have survived having touched the body of a man with a bad spirit, and therefore it had to be burned to ashes to allow them to continue their journey safely.

They also, for their own preservation, had needed to go without food and shelter for two days, alone, to fully rid themselves of the ill spirit in the body they had transported. The difficulty lay, he explained simply, in the fact that the blanket and body were wet and needed an especially hot fire and extra burning time.

Luc's stomach heaved again; he stumbled for a distance and then righted himself. What Mathew had told him was helpful, but why hadn't he simply explained this prior to abandoning him in the night? Mathew offered that the uncertainty and fear Luc had experienced further had cleansed him. Luc now only wanted to leave the area and throw himself into a rushing spring and wash his body and soul—although apparently his soul was now very clean—before proceeding. He didn't want to hear the explanation and was relieved to know his friend hadn't turned on him. Someday he would be interested in food again.

Moving away from the pyre, the pair, weak yet determined, mounted their horses. Overwrought and silent, they relocated slowly and set up a place to camp. They brewed strong black tea and sugar and had small amounts of dense bread and dried beef. In an attempt to lighten the mood, Luc wanted to know whether this was different tea from what Mathew had served him a couple of nights ago. He received no reply, only a small smile from his companion.

"With this act we've helped complete your sister's journey too," Mathew offered, after a long, comfortable rest. "We can now focus on our mission and not look over our shoulders."

"She'll never know the half of the situation." Luc was gaining momentum again for the big-picture purpose, his youthful resilience propelling him forward in his mission. Giselle's plight was secondary again.

Without conversation or hesitation, Mathew guided Luc to the slope, where their cargo was stored and where Lewis lived. They concurred they had to make up some time, both wanting their full share of the agreed-upon payment at the end. There were other caches to pick up and men to meet with, all of which Luc and Tristan had arranged.

Luc's thoughts drifted ahead to meeting up with Malcolm Rast and Stuart Sheen. It had been days since he had given the two any consideration. In his opinion, they'd been given a large amount of the soft side of this job, mostly traveling in one of the automobiles in Tristan's newly acquired fleet. They spent very little time on a trail on horseback or with a wagon and cart. Tristan had high expectations of them, and they certainly had the passion to get ahead and work hard, but one thing struck Luc as very odd. They rarely could be separated. They communicated with few words—sometimes no words—and preferred jobs where they could work together.

Considering Tristan's reverence for self-made independence, Luc was amazed the Atlantic lads had gained his favor. Perhaps it was due to that one thing Luc couldn't claim: knowledge of ships and sailing. Their knowledge wasn't as vast or sophisticated as the Kaye family's, but they definitely knew their way around vessels of many sizes, as well as shipyards and docks and, if what was spun in their charismatic stories was true, the Atlantic Ocean. When Malcolm and Stuart were on the job, they were quiet and introverted. But there was no shortage of tales from the pair of raconteurs when they were relaxing among peers. They brought to life vivid scenes of fishing and life by the sea but no words of love and family.

Luc snapped out of his thoughts with their arrival upon the familiar slope at Lewis's place. He urged his horse along with Mathew, who was calm but always looking around, to the point of distraction for Luc. Couldn't he move a little more quickly? They needed to make up time. There was no sign of Lewis at first, but as soon as they dismounted outside the shack, he appeared from nowhere, behind them. He looked worn out. They exchanged greetings and proceeded to gather the bottles, jugs, and jars.

Lewis, needing to rest from his wheezing and persistent coughing, asked innocuously, "You boys always send scouts out first?" Luc scrutinized the man's face. Lewis continued. "Those lads you were here with the first time came by a couple of days ago. Said you sent them to make sure I'd cooperate. Then they rode off." Luc and Mathew froze. Why were Rast and Sheen not miles away? Luc's uneasiness with respect to the pair was heightened. Without exchanging words—only glances—he and Mathew simultaneously picked up the pace.

# CHAPTER 26
# LAKE ONTARIO

Settled comfortably on the soft mahogany leather in the backseat of his automobile, Tristan quietly organized his thoughts regarding the upcoming shipment. The new undertaking was moving along well, and he felt confident in his choice of men and route. His car was the second of three on the road, with two members of his security staff ahead and the bankers bringing up the rear. He sipped from a slim, elegant silver flask. There was a quality in the brew from the bush that couldn't be matched. He would have to ensure the new producers kept it top quality and didn't balk at the exclusive arrangement; after all they were getting paid top dollar.

This stretch of Ontario road would be especially relaxing, as he had opted to be chauffeured; although Tristan had earned his stature in life, he didn't always indulge in the benefits. Fields of young corn went by, the skies filled with black crows. Sometimes the corn was a mere two feet from the road, making the road a tunnel, somewhat darker. Then the open landscape, with its mellow hills and greenery, would return, allowing his thoughts to expand with the view.

He would need to visit the shipyard in Montreal soon. There were still the reliable old routes to tend to; not all of his attention should be directed toward the new venture.

There also were vessels that had been loaded and were ready to return to Halifax, where they would take on rum from the Caribbean, obtained with his seafaring fleet. Then the Canadian brew and rum would be hastily transported to the eastern US ports—that and the precious European liquor. His father never would have done this—he did lightly joke about the possibilities but never took the leap. And Seamus had been more pliable and cooperative than Tristan was.

If Rast and Sheen were as capable on land as they had proved to be in shipping, all would be well. There was just something he couldn't put his finger on with the pair.

Tristan also knew Luc would notice the shift of focus onto them, but he was hoping Luc was smart enough to know he was merely being cautious and keeping them under observation. Their potential was great, but tandem thinking among henchmen usually didn't bode well. He had seen it in weaker men, but this was somewhat odd, as Rast and Sheen weren't weak spirited. Indeed, they had shown guts and no sign of resistance toward the game plan or hesitation with jobs.

The journey to the meeting place at the top of Lake Ontario included a few stops in smaller communities and villages, so Tristan could get a feel for where the local brew came from and test the quality. Everywhere people were enjoying spirits at home and away from home, and many were producing fine liquor. All was going well. During the evening portions of the trip, the hillsides often showed the dotted glows of small fires as locals cooked mash. It was the nation's pastime, and they needed management and direction regarding the business end of it.

He had good men working for him; the situation with Luc's sister would prove what Luc was made of. Tristan didn't doubt he would stay steady with the plan—meaning, business as usual—and also come through for his sister. Giselle's character was impressive; her strength and intelligence made him wish he could have spent more time in her company. At first, he thought it was because her charm reminded him of Madeline, but no, it was that she reminded him of himself—kindred spirits possibly. How could he see her again?

The village of Loren certainly had proved to be more than interesting. Not only had he seen Father Gaston after so many years, but also the sudden complication of the murder of Luc's brother-in-law and the subsequent dilemma of Giselle feeling afraid due to the behavior of the murderer's son were curious and compelling.

# CHAPTER 27
# FOUR DAYS PRIOR

At the sandbar on the Helle, crouched in the bushes, Rast and Sheen hatched a plan. Fate had planted them at the right place at the right time. Spying on coworkers and listening in on conversations they weren't meant to hear came naturally to them; slyness was a virtue in their world.

"If we figure out whose body they're carting into the bush, we might have some leverage to make ourselves a spot in the organization," Sheen assumed out loud.

They couldn't connect a mysterious body with Luc and Mathew's trip to Lewis's, so they presumed Luc was hiding something. They had lingered in Loren longer than they were supposed to, hoping to find out more about Luc's role in Tristan's hierarchy and see whether they could rattle him a little by letting him know they were prepared to do anything to advance up the chain. They knew he did business by the sandbar at the river and happened to see him and Mathew making some physical adjustments to their lifeless cargo.

Rast countered with another idea. "Anyway, if this gets us nowhere, we can always make them both disappear and say we saw one kill the other and try to run off with the booze. Then we'll bring the load to Tristan at the lake and save the day."

Sheen preferred the pressure tactic, as they'd already overheard talk from a man named Will Frank at the local watering hole that Tristan may have shown interest in Luc's sister. Could that make their boss vulnerable to not wanting any dirt on her or her brother surfacing? Maybe not yet, but if a relationship developed, it would. And Luc himself definitely was vulnerable now.

Following an experienced guide through the bush undetected wasn't easy. Every muscle in their bodies tensed without respite as they tried to avoid making the faintest snap or noise in the brush. It was good that the Frenchman was noisier and less stealthy; he unknowingly assisted them. The sight of Mathew and Luc in the bog, not far off the trail, placing the wrapped body in the sinking marsh and weighing it down with stones captivated them. When it was apparent the two men weren't proceeding directly to Lewis's, Rast and Sheen's elation could hardly be tempered.

They needed to get there first to ascertain if it was, by chance, Lewis's body they were sinking in the bog and make sure the brew was still available should they opt to heist it. Their plan could change slightly, but obtaining facts never hurt, and the plan was to push Luc out one way or another.

Lewis was positioned near the first cave storage area. Silenced by the awareness of approaching riders, he hung back in the shadows, hoping his blasted cough wouldn't give him away. He had succumbed to a fever and had experienced difficulty breathing over the past few days. He knew the signs, but he couldn't worry about that right now; he was busy listening to the lads passing by on horseback, heading to his shack. He heard them almost excitedly discussing seeing the Frenchman and the guide sinking a body. He had been expecting Luc and Mathew soon to pick up the load. What the hell were they up to with a body near his land? Good information to keep to himself.

This whole takeover didn't make him happy; he was helpless, even though he likely would make more money. He didn't need a lot of money, however, or want a different life, especially now with the illness that had struck his family. It was too late, really; when he was younger, he may have refused and fought, but now he was just tired and existing—not living. On the first visit, he had noticed a bit of a rift between the three—maybe not a rift but a glaring difference in personalities and a bond between the two who sounded like Irishmen.

Lewis followed them to his shack and appeared behind them, catching them off guard. They said Luc wanted to know if all was ready. He went along with this friendly facade; they couldn't get rid of him, as he had the recipes for the brew in his head and the skill in his hands. They left as unexpectedly and quickly as they'd appeared.

In the fading light, Lewis settled in his shack with a meal of rabbit stew and fresh bread. He would have to make a trip to a doctor if his cough and fever didn't let up. He had the next batch cooking in the stills, so all he had to do was monitor it for the next few weeks.

He finished his meal, and even though it was still light, he lay in his bed. After no more than five minutes, he heard an energetic pounding of hooves approaching—only one set, though. He looked outside to see a familiar customer, someone who consumed expensive brandy and port on a regular basis but couldn't resist the deep haze induced by good brew. It was the mayor of Loren, Maxwell Loren himself.

"Lewis, you look like hell," Maxwell greeted him.

"I'll be all right."

"I hope your spirits are in better shape!" jested the mayor. He didn't really care about Lewis's health; they both knew better. "I've ridden later than I'd planned, but if I get what I need and make haste, I'll be home before dark. I know all the shortcuts to this place."

Lewis went off to get the mayor's jugs and, upon returning, explained briefly about the takeover. The mayor didn't really listen closely past the part about how he should still be able to supply him but might need a bit of notice in the future, until he mentioned Tristan Kaye. The local gossip had been rampant with the appearance of Tristan in the village and then his mysterious visit to their church, followed by his reunion with Father Gaston and calling on Giselle Reicher. To further unsettle the mayor, he didn't particularly like the insinuations from a man who had been in the home, his friend Will Frank. Will insinuated Giselle had caught the eye of the mogul. It was nothing overt, just that he obviously found her engaging. Will said he couldn't tell if she might feel the same.

Will only wanted the best for Giselle, but Maxwell wasn't sure how he felt about that. He often had cursed the universe for the fact that such a lovely, intelligent wife had been acquired by Reicher—a simple blacksmith who couldn't offer her more than mere adequacy. She fascinated Maxwell like no other creature. Unfortunately, Maxwell was comfortable with conflicting emotions and experienced nearly every emotion each day.

He could harbor the most critical, condescending thoughts about his friends yet warmly interact with them as if he felt nothing but admiration. He thought all successful men talked out of both sides of their mouths.

Maxwell grew tired of Lewis's story of his plight, dismissed it, and proceeded to discuss whatever came into his mind while they shared a shot of brew prior to his mounting his horse. He couldn't resist the opportunity to toy with the simple man a bit. "Lewis, I like the simplicity of your operation here, with nothing but the crudest of amenities."

"I doubt that, Mr. Mayor." Lewis wasn't about to bite the bait.

Loren continued to ramble about how he envied the bushman's quiet life in solitude, as currently the town was buzzing with gossip over the disappearance of the deceased farmer's widow and now his son too. The rumor was that young Ivan was as crazy as his father and had been stalking Josef Reicher's widow.

Lewis couldn't comment on that. "You know I never leave my place unless I need to get something," he explained.

The strong moonshine was affecting both of them. Relaxed and indifferent, Lewis revealed that he had heard the lads discussing having seen a body dumped in the bog. And they also had overheard an astounding conversation between the Frenchman and the Algonquin guide that may have involved the Frenchman's sister, the widow of the blacksmith.

"Sorry?" Maxwell got to his feet and then decided not to seem too startled, despite his inebriation. "Is that just speculation, man? Are you telling me God's truth?"

Lewis was now the one not interested the other man's concerns: "I know what I heard."

Maxwell rose above the glow of the moonshine to pay special attention without being obvious. What the hell would Giselle and Luc be doing with a body? With neither man wanting to pursue the realities of the topic, they laughed it off awkwardly in an attempt to minimize it, and Maxwell set off for home.

He was anything but relaxed now; perhaps he was even somewhat giddy that fate had set out more trump cards in his favor for the taking. If any of this were true, he could wield it against that bastard Tristan Kaye.

The Montreal mogul's new "interest" and her brother were very close, and this could provide Maxwell with an advantage. Perhaps he could persuade Tristan to reign in his designs on Giselle in exchange for Maxwell not exposing Luc. He rode faster than was safe in the darkness, oblivious to any perils on the trail, as he needed to get home and do some investigating.

# CHAPTER 28
# DISEASE

Deep in the bush, Luc listened to the shallow breathing of his friend, who slept by the fire. He saw sweat on Mathew's face despite the cool night air. He had given him willow-bark tea to cool his fever and ease the pain in his chest and back from coughing.

The past three days had wreaked havoc on the guide, beginning with a cough, but he hardly could catch his breath now and was too fatigued to ride even in daylight hours. Not knowing if it was influenza or some kind of plague, Luc was beside himself while deciding what to do for his friend.

Luc's mind was a tangled, frantic web of fears. How could he help Mathew? How would he get the load delivered on time for Tristan? Already they were behind schedule. Worst of all, what if he got sick too? He hoped Mathew still wasn't terrified of his contact with young Ivan's body. Luc couldn't be certain, as Mathew was too weak to speak much. He made sure his friend was comfortable and then sat nearby and attempted to calm his mind and think logically.

Mathew broke the silence. "You have to go without me. We're near enough to my home. You'll lose half a day if you take me there, but I'll die if I try to make the trip. Or you could shoot me and leave me here." He delivered this humor with barely any oxygen. Luc wondered about the Algonquin's faith and culture and felt a bit encouraged knowing his family was nearby. Although his home was only a half day's journey away, every half day was precious traveling time.

Luc and Mathew were worn down, but Luc was going to keep on. He had to take his losses in time now, get Mathew to his wife and family, and then try to make up the lost time, sparing nothing. He resolved he would die trying, as this opportunity wouldn't come around again.

Some of the other collection teams had sent out a few men to find them, as the evidence of the delay had spread concern. Others had money riding on this trip too and didn't take lightly the fact that they hadn't yet returned. Fortunately, when a group of riders found Luc and Mathew, Luc explained the situation, and with no other options, two men stayed with them to assist in delivering Mathew to his home. Two others headed back to where their load was to carry on with a newly developed contingency plan.

A half day of travel brought them to the lake where Mathew lived. He couldn't lie down; the coughing was worse that way. The smell of cooked stew and bread baking was overwhelming for Luc and even Mathew, who was too ill to eat. Luc couldn't make sense of why he hadn't become ill too, especially since he'd been weakened during the purification process Mathew had inflicted on them. Maybe those times, years ago, when his sister was a nurse and had insisted he get some inoculations of some sort had paid off. He had fought her on that, saying it was a waste of time. She had said it would prevent some kind of horrible illnesses, and whatever Mathew and Lewis had was definitely horrible.

Luc once again dug deeply—emotionally—to enable himself to leave his friend and carry on with the mission. Giselle flitted into his thoughts, but he forced them into the back of his consciousness. He said good-bye to his friend, not knowing if he'd ever see him again. If Mathew survived the illness, they would surely meet. Mathew explained, as best he could, about the rest of the journey. Luc could write, so he laboriously penned on crude paper all of Mathew's instructions.

There were perils and challenges on the road ahead, but Luc felt confident, and the desire to lead and be successful took over his soul. He and the others left the Algonquin community with the load, and within a day, they met up with some of the other contacts. They had to cover a lot of ground in a few days, as they should have been at Lake Ontario already. More than a few days' delay would cause Tristan some concern but nothing serious. Past a few weeks, he would send out some of his staff, who would ride fast and expect a damn good explanation, taking over if necessary.

The weather was on Luc's side, and his energy was returning. The Ontario landscape was beautiful, and the roads, as crude as they were—more like trails really—weren't well traveled but showed no major obstacles.

At night the men thwarted the insects with layers of stinking bear grease applied to their skin. There was no time to bathe in the sparkling streams and small waterfalls in the shale. And they had no desire to do anything but get the load to the lake. They bedded down for short periods at night—just enough hours to stave off exhaustion.

Then they saw them—the landmarks where they were instructed to stop and hide the load away from the road. Mathew had said they would be rock formations that looked like two bears standing and facing each other on either side of the road. At that point they were to send two riders ahead, as Lake Ontario was a few hours away, to make sure the time was right and the laker was ready to be loaded.

Luc and another fellow from the Opeongo area rode swiftly; the whole time, Luc was rehearsing his explanation for Tristan—if Tristan were there. There shouldn't be any reason he wouldn't be, but frustration and anxiety had consumed Luc since the first day of the trip. He smelled the lake: the combination of moist air, rotting weeds, fresh fish, and wet beaches. When they were resting the horses, they heard the sounds of waterbirds and sensed the closeness. This leg of their journey really could be finished soon.

The pair mounted again and rode to an open spot that overlooked the lake. It was late afternoon, and the instructions Mathew had provided laid out exactly what they would see at their first real sighting of the lake. They were to travel a few hundred yards east off the road and look for a building—a well-kept cabin—and were to wait in it or near it for Tristan.

They didn't have to wait, as Tristan appeared from inside with several men. He studied Luc for a second.

Luc knew better than to speak first; he would let Tristan put this together himself and not interrupt.

"Where the hell is Mathew?" Tristan looked anything but happy.

"Sick and possibly not even alive. We got him back to his home. I couldn't leave him in the bush in his condition." Luc was steady in his speech.

"Anyone else missing or sick?"

"No, and the load is intact." Luc knew that would be the next question.

"All right," Tristan said unceremoniously, "we have to get busy and load the laker. It's ready, and we're seriously behind. I'm meeting Tom Carter at a port nearby. From there we'll be taking his private boat to a port in Monroe County, New York. Luc, pay attention to balancing the load, as the ship looks like it could be top heavy and might have listing issues in bad weather. I'm leaving this with you now and will tell everyone you're in charge. See you in Rochester." With that, Tristan departed.

Luc smiled inwardly; Tristan wouldn't be asking him to hand over the reins.

There was so much more to tell Tristan, but now wasn't the time. Loading the goods in the cover of darkness and setting across the lake were paramount. By late tonight they could be done stocking the ship. The weather looked fine, as far as they could see.

Tristan had arranged for assistance with the loading, as getting bush-weary men to do it never had proved
speedy in the past. By midnight the steamer was ready
and had set off across the lake. The men accompanying
the load were shown to their sleeping quarters. Luc was
impressed; there were very respectable-looking cabins
above the cargo area. Malcolm Rast and Stuart Sheen
surfaced but avoided Luc; he made a mental note to
deal with them at the end of this trip.

Tristan, as planned, had met with Tom Carter,
and they'd discussed price and volume. As suspected,
Carter had bought everything. He would hand over
the cash on the other side of the lake upon the ship's
unloading in the United States.

Luc was too excited to sleep. The night was
calm, so the ship skimmed over the lake. He remembered Tristan's comment about the load's weight
distribution—a casual observation likely supported
by his expertise in shipbuilding. He often had commented that the vessels that brought rum from the
Caribbean were mostly ones he never would be caught
dead on. Luc stepped onto the deck and enjoyed the
warm night air. The sparkly, diamond-delicate white
crests of the waves were hypnotic. Seagulls swooped
around the laker near the shores.

In the morning, they docked at a small, discreet
port and unloaded into waiting trucks. There would

be no carts and horses on this side. Tristan said they
could expect vehicles at home next time. He would
reroute the small suppliers' loads to more mainstream roads, as accessibility was growing every day
to accommodate automobiles. And they also would
do more by truck. He commented that even where
Rast and Sheen were from they trucked loads.

Luc had been trying to observe the relationship
between Tristan and the Atlantic lads. Conversation
was minimal; they said hardly anything when Tristan
was around yet exchanged hostile glances and comments when he wasn't.

They didn't speak to Luc; it was obvious even to
others. He couldn't figure it out, except perhaps they
didn't like the fact that he was more outgoing and
knowledgeable regarding his job. Why were they act-
ing as if they didn't know him now?

Malcolm and Stuart accompanied Tristan to Tom
Carter's bank with the financial men, along with three
others. Luc was relieved they wouldn't have access to
the cash and were just there to protect those who did.

They all would be taking the laker back to
Ontario, relieved, and the men would have time to
talk. Luc tested the waters by asking Malcolm what he
thought of the boat.

"I've been on bigger. It's a steady one, though," he
offered.

"We're fortunate to have this opportunity," Luc ventured but received no response.

The weather wasn't as calm on this trip, so he decided he would tend to a few of his comrades who were feeling seasick. The listing was a bit of a problem. Oddly enough, Malcolm and Stuart didn't pipe up about that, especially since they were so experienced with vessels.

Tristan broke Luc's thoughts with a request to speak to him privately. They met in the cabin reserved for Tristan's meeting with his banker's representatives. They were alone now, though.

Tristan went straight to the point. "What are your plans? How soon can you come back to Montreal? I know you have the weight of your sister's mental health on you right now."

Luc felt it was quite intuitive that Tristan sensed Giselle might be in need, even without his knowing the whole unbelievable story. He wondered if, perhaps, Tristan was thinking of Giselle and not him.

"I need to stop at her village and check on her," Luc replied. "She's been suffering from unbelievable stress, and I left her there alone with it in order to see this job through. There are some things I need to discuss with you that you might find a better time for. We aren't at the end of the job yet—maybe when we settle up in Montreal."

"Did something happen?" Tristan asked. "Something other than the son of that Hauffe man frightening her?"

Luc was now convinced that Tristan had been giving Giselle and her situation quite a bit of thought. It wouldn't be a problem telling him about young Ivan and the real reason behind the delay. It wasn't as if they were all schoolteachers. He was now curious, however, about Tristan's interest in Giselle. He replied simply to the direct question. "Yes."

"My wish is to see more of her," Tristan revealed. "That may or may not cause a ripple in the ranks of business, but I'm willing to see what happens. I know you're thinking your brother-in-law's passing was quite recent, and I'm sure she feels the same, but I see a lot of myself in her—a like-mindedness."

"True enough, and I guess time is what she needs. She plans on going back to work for the VON and also is talking of the National Women's Council. She'd like to support their cause through activism and volunteering. That wasn't something Josef felt they could make work in their life together, so she didn't, but now...I don't think she'll be stopped." Luc didn't think this would faze Tristan, and it didn't. He suspected his boss was harboring feelings for his sister, undoubtedly, but the inevitability of her discovering the darker side of their lives left him unsettled.

But that had to be put off for now. His craving for success didn't let him dwell on his sister's matters of the heart.

Tristan smiled. "Both are good causes. Times are changing."

They dropped the topic, as the ship was approaching the Canadian shore of the lake, and they needed to get their belongings to prepare to disembark.

"Can I take a couple of weeks before I return to Montreal?" Luc asked.

"Certainly," Tristan told him.

As promised, Luc was paid, and he began his journey to Loren on horseback, along with those who were returning in the same direction. His thoughts were calmer now because the job was done, and Tristan had invited him back to Montreal, but now surfacing were the disturbing images of Giselle before he had left, as well as those of young Ivan— not to mention the purification journey Mathew had taken him on.

The trip back to Loren gave him several days to process everything that had happened. He stopped at the sandbar on the Helle, where he first had met Mathew, and contemplated going to Mathew's home first, as he didn't know whether his friend had survived. But this time he put Giselle first, as strong as she was. The river was unchanged, of course, and he felt a sense of peace as he approached the road to his sister's house.

Luc slowly made his way to Giselle's door; the fragrant flowers of her garden were outrageously beautiful. There was no hint whatsoever of what had happened at the house. He heard quiet conversation—calm, pleasant talk floating out of the open window. He passed through the house to the back veranda.

Father Gaston looked pleased to see him, and Giselle, startled, greeted him as she did the day of the funeral. It was surreal; Luc was impressed with how easily she could restore normalcy to chaos. It was good to be in her home and see her safe and calm. One emotion that hadn't surfaced for him in the past weeks was relief—the realization that now there would be no more stalking, unnerving encounters, or fear for Giselle. She could reclaim her life.

"I'm talking with your sister about her relocating to Montreal. The girls are there with Aline and her family. The acceptance on their part is taken care of. Why stay here?" Father Gaston was asking Luc, but Giselle responded.

"I haven't decided how I feel about that," she countered. "I see the sense, theoretically, but maybe I'm not done living here yet. Do I want to remember this place as somewhere I was chased away from? In fear?"

Luc was wondering how the obvious subject would come out. He was waiting.

Father Gaston didn't disappoint him. "Ivan Hauffe's older son has mysteriously disappeared. His mother and younger brother have been missing for weeks. The farm is deserted. All of this is sad and unfortunate. Your family almost was destroyed, and another one completely vanished. I've encouraged Giselle to stop trying to make sense of Josef's death— stop trying to figure out why. We should help her move on to the next part of her life."

"I'll let her decide what's best for her, Father. Giselle by no means lacks intelligence. We appreciate your concern, so please don't take offense. What are your thoughts on what happened to the Hauffe family? Are there any clues?" Luc had to ask and was hoping his sister hadn't already pressed the priest too much about it.

"Some have said Mr. Hauffe was dangerously mentally ill," Father Gaston offered, "and perhaps the affliction was passed down. Irrational and ill-tempered to the point of madness, they may have been. Some say evil. Either way their illness went undiagnosed and untreated. I know Hauffe struggled financially to feed the family, and the times I visited them, he was downright tyrannical. Who knows what motivates an unhealthy mind and soul to take drastic action? This has been a tragic set of circumstances for our brothers and sisters of the community, Catholic and non-Catholic alike, and it's time to go forward. I'm hoping you'll suggest to your sister that taking the girls to Aline's, in Montreal, makes the most sense. We need to put all this behind us."

It never ceased to amaze Luc how smooth the priest was, and somehow entire segments of the population absolutely lingered on every word that men of the cloth uttered, waiting for the holy men to speak and judge. Luc felt it might be prudent to keep his own comments brief and somewhat vague.

"I appreciate your thoughts, Father, and will give some consideration to them."

Father Gaston raised an eyebrow, as if surprised this was all he was getting out of the young man. He glanced toward Giselle, who had been silent. She resisted telling them she felt like a prop, a nonexistent article they talked about as if it weren't present.

She made her decision unexpectedly. "I do feel it's best to relocate—not to hide or forget but to evolve and grow. I feel it's ideal with my sister living there, and it'll be easier to pursue my VON career again. I can work while the girls are in school. Luc and I will have to decide what to do with the household effects. Some of the items in Josef's shop I will want to keep. Mostly I want the change—just a change."

A deep quietness comfortably enveloped the three. The house had changed, the atmosphere altered by pain and fear but not beaten altogether. Strength of character was the resounding sentiment.

Satisfied he had given sound advice, Father Gaston departed. He would be visiting Montreal occasionally too. It was obvious to him how things were really going. He had heard the rumors from the other priests, some from Montreal, that Luc's boss was interested in Giselle. Tristan Kaye was one of the biggest contributors to the diocese. Yes, his career was questionable, but his loyalty to the church had served the priests, bishops, and Lord quite well. St. Louis de France Church was a jewel.

Father Gaston would have to navigate this carefully; he needed to support his valued acquaintance regarding his "interest" but must not be perceived by his congregation as condoning a recent widow from his flock taking up with a "gangster." Perhaps he needed to disappear for a while. But cowardice wasn't his style. He had said his words to the widow—the right words, he believed. Now he had to temper his actions. Tristan hadn't spoken with him about the matter or his intentions. He wondered whether Luc had picked up on his boss's interest in his sister. For that matter he wondered whether Giselle had any idea. He said a prayer and then an extra one to prepare himself for a visit to the mayor.

Over the next week, Luc and Giselle organized the family belongings. Several local businesses bought most of Josef's tools. Giselle received several offers on the property, with none of the prospective buyers having any intention of carrying on with blacksmithing. Josef's business was disappearing, which was unfathomable to her. His craft had died with him in this village.

The upcoming trip to Montreal was many things for Giselle. She was anticipating seeing her daughters and sister and reveling in female company to talk and cry and laugh. When she was around Luc, Father Gaston, the bankers, the solicitor, and the doctor, she had to be stoic and keep her emotions in check. She was tired of male company. That notion made her laugh somewhat. They all thought she was oblivious to Mr. Kaye's interest in her. Why else would he have visited her home? It wasn't to spend time with Luc, his employee. She wasn't sure what she thought of it. She wasn't capable of forming a serious romantic bond right now, and she knew Mr. Kaye was aware of that. She admired that; she sensed he had a realistic view of her, and she understood that maybe they were like-minded. That was as much as she could muster at the moment. This was her time to ground herself and get back to working as a nurse. She needed the distraction and the purposefulness.

Giselle sent a letter to her sister, informing her of her decision to move to Montreal. Luc was relieved; now he could relax with his sister and nieces living near him. He would have no worries about leaving them alone while he was on the job. He was anxious to get back to Montreal, as he knew Tristan was waiting for the proper opportunity to give him feedback about how the smuggling operation had gone. Would this go his way?

# CHAPTER 29
# THE VISIT

The mayor opened his door cautiously. This was an unexpected knock and visit. Father Gaston stood looking at him with a dignified air—perfectly still in the moonlight and cool breeze.

"Come in, Father," Maxwell said steadily, although he was completely caught off guard.

"I'm hoping you have time for a conversation this evening." As the priest entered the home, he took in the lush surroundings, especially the artwork.

"Of course. What's on your mind?" Maxwell replied and then motioned toward the tea trolley—a gesture intended for the ever-present housekeeper.

"The mental welfare of the village is on my mind, quite frankly. This past spring and summer tested everyone's faith and fears. As you know, I worry about my flock, and quite often I'm the first contact for the authorities when something terrible happens...," he said, his voice trailing off.

The mayor's face dimmed ever so slightly, but he hoped the faint evening lighting was in his favor. "And the authorities asked about me?"

"No, but I like to seek thoughts and opinions from everyone I can. I have to make some sense of everything that's happened for the congregation, you know. The more perspectives I'm familiar with, the better I can comfort them."

"Of course," Maxwell offered and then realized after a bit of a silence that he was expected to discuss the murder and the disappearances. "I don't have much to offer," he said. "It's all been very tragic—Mrs. Reicher left alone and then the Hauffe family vanishing. Who knows where they are?"

The priest was direct. "You're aware there were situations of intense fear on Giselle's part due to outward hostility from young Ivan, yes? Do you have any thoughts regarding why he may have blamed her... for something? You must know her fairly well, as she was your good friend's wife. Come to think of it, sir, I find it a bit interesting that you haven't visited her in her time of need."

"I have, but she was never there." Maxwell was uncomfortable, looking away; he hated lying to a priest. Father Gaston must have been closer to Giselle than he suspected. How would he know he hadn't been there?

"Mr. Loren, if a man has designs on a widow, it's best left undetected for at least a year," Father Gaston stated boldly.

Maxwell had consumed a lot of brandy that evening, and even though the tea had been presented, he still opted for brandy. He rubbed his face briskly. "If you're suggesting I have designs on Giselle, that's both bold and tiring. I've been alone a long time. Of course, it's crossed my mind; I see no reason to keep that from you. I realize it offends you morally, but legally it holds no repercussions. What exactly are you thinking you can do about it, good Father?" Maxwell didn't see what was coming next.

"I'm referring to Tristan Kaye." Father Gaston certainly had gleaned an interesting perspective with his bluff; what Maxwell had said was practically a confession.

The mayor stiffened and looked away. He had heard some gossip but didn't want to believe it. "That pompous Irishman from Montreal? The showoff?" Maxwell was feeling angry, drunk, and brave. "I'll thank you not to say his name in my home! Furthermore, Giselle never would take to a man so utterly open about his criminal activity. I won't have it!"

"I understand, Maxwell. Although I'm a priest, I am a man too, but you don't realize who you're dealing with. I would advise you strongly to stay out of Tristan Kaye's way if it came to an in-person encounter. That's all I have to offer you. I will say good night."

Father Gaston showed himself out, as Maxwell seemed to be feeling unsteady. He likely would sleep near the empty brandy bottle. He did slide onto the couch but didn't surrender to the alcohol or the rude information put before him.

Maxwell turned to his beloved graveyard painting. The monks had their backs to him but he was certain, in his haze, they were turning to listen. "How can an Irish thug, likely uneducated, turn her head? It's more than ridiculous, it's a bloody crime! No one knows the connections I have and the reach to make them wish they had never met me! I could reduce every man in this county to ruins if I decided. There are people who owe me! I will set this situation on the proper course, damn them all to hell, if necessary!" He spoke to the walls, studied the abby on the wall, and announced to the dead that he had far more power than the Irishman, and he would call in his markers this very night, if necessary, to eliminate this problem. Sleep took him in the middle of his rant, and there he stayed until dawn.

# CHAPTER 30
# THE PLAN

Malcolm Rast and Stuart Sheen had been keeping low profiles for the purposes of observation. Now that the Lake Ontario job was done, they would head back to Montreal with Tristan, but he had asked them to check on Luc first at his sister's village. He didn't reveal why Luc wouldn't be going back with the rest immediately, but they dutifully didn't inquire and in fact found it difficult not to smile, as this facilitated their scheme very nicely.

Luc had left for the village before them and was unaware they had been sent—even better. They could take a day or two to do some sleuthing regarding the situation with the body and remain undetected. They were instructed to stop at Giselle Reicher's home on behalf of Tristan, which would provide them with the perfect cover. If there were anything to discover, it would keep Luc from returning or eject him from Tristan's inner circle, at which point they would move in like sharks.

The pair arrived in Loren and headed to the hotel tavern for beer and any conversation they could get with some locals. They were more than pleased to see a full house moving along enthusiastically with a Saturday evening. They positioned themselves at an end of the bar that seemed busiest. Charming ale-soaked tales and interactions with strangers were their specialty. Rast and Sheen could kill hours with this pastime.

A stumbling, well-dressed man approached them, obviously past his sensible consumption limit. He had a glass of spirits in one hand and the bottle in the other. Having gotten drunk at home the previous night, there would be no dispute from the barkeep if he carried on a bit tonight; it was only a problem if he dirtied the establishment several evenings in a row—mayor or not. He eyed the pair cautiously and stated the obvious. "Haven't I seen you two before?" It was a question and an answer conveyed simultaneously in a drunken comment. The brandy haze penetrated briefly. He could fight it all right. He could navigate another full glass before he would succumb and go down.

So could Rast and Sheen; alcohol was their muse and weapon of choice—a strange liquid bond, it seemed, smoothly and elegantly slipping around from behind them unnoticed, securing their audience for hours.

They joined him, three black hearts pumping as one, each recognizing and relishing the like-minded urge to drink and spin yarns. The conversation that unfolded struck all of them as the winning hand. If fate shifted them all in the same direction, nothing could stop them.

It started with small talk. Then—after making certain everyone around them heard them say they'd been working on the railway that had been expanded through the valley—Rast announced, "Have you heard of Mr. Kaye, then? Mr. Tristan Kaye. We are some of the boys that do jobs for him and his restaurant business. It's a thriving business he has, there. You must have heard of him? You being a local businessman and all."

Upon receiving this information, Maxwell, barely able to speak properly, steadied himself and slowly spat out his seething hatred for the man. "You mean that bastard who calls himself an exporter?"

The two were absorbing the reaction. Rast offered an opportunity for the mayor to continue. "Are you sure you mean Tristan Kaye, sir?"

"That's the character, I'm certain. The bane of my life at the moment if you must know." The Irish kingpin had possibly had caused the disarming of his best game play ever: his chance at securing a fine woman, the one he always had wanted. Giselle was now free of that boring, laboring husband whose company he'd endured for years, all those long, painful hours of contemplating the future and listening to him speak of Giselle and their children—the blacksmith's integrity making Maxwell more ill than a plague.

The brandy was spurring him on to a long soliloquy of rage, self-pity, and self-indulgent ranting. "I'm growing extremely short on patience with the man. I have a conducted myself in a dignified manner all my life and what do I get in return? Overlooked? For whom? I have played this out in the most organized manner, yet I am met with stupidity time and time again. I can't win. I am certain I need to formulate a different course of action..." His words were running together but nonetheless intrigued the pair.

Rast and Sheen listened dutifully at first and, without a word to each other, knowingly cheered him on to tell more when he began to fade. They'd been exposed to hundreds of storytellers in taverns and were artfully sorting the fabricated from the factual. Maxwell Loren's wealth and power—if they were as vast as he implied—and his grudge against Tristan could provide them with support for their plan.

Timing was everything in their line of work. After Maxwell had gotten comfortable with them, they offered up their thoughts as to how they might be able to help one another. They were in Tristan's trust—valuable employees with knowledge of his business. They didn't give up too much but made it clear they might have something on Luc that might implicate his sister. Sheen piped up. "Mr. Loren we can definitely help each other. If we come up with an idea or two together we will be further ahead than not."

Rast wished Sheen wouldn't bother talking sometimes but at least Loren wasn't a sharp audience at the moment. They tried not to show Maxwell how desperate they were to surpass Luc in the ranks of Tristan's empire, but he felt their passion. Not much could hide a criminal's desire to win.

They all needed to sober up by the next morning, rally, and finalize the plan. Rast and Sheen would return to Montreal with something to work on. Maxwell could join them anytime. They could carry on the status quo, for a while, smugly confident and knowing. But at the right time, Mr. Kaye may be presented with some information that might make him want to buy them off. The more they drank the more solid the plan seemed.

# CHAPTER 31
# LEAVING

Reuniting with her daughters at her sister's home was exactly what Giselle needed to propel her into a good, safe world again. Her preparation for departing from Loren had taken several weeks, and she completed it with a clear sense of direction. This was for the best; her home had become something other than a sanctuary. She had to arrange for storage in Montreal for many things she wasn't prepared to live without.

Prior to leaving, Giselle received confirmation from the Victorian Order of Nurses that she could be employed again and simply needed to let them know where she wanted to work. Her days would now at least hold some hours in which she didn't ruminate and seize up with guilt and flashbacks.

Giselle's mind held very graphic images, and she was determined to keep them out. She was aware Luc was observing her closely and worrying. He had arranged to be in Loren for a couple of weeks and stay with her to assist with the move. They had agreed not to discuss what had happened on the property with young Ivan until she was safely in Montreal. Her mind had a strange way of reconciling the death of the young man. If he hadn't died outside of the house, she never would have been able to be inside it, even briefly. This was a line of definition for her.

But she was very open to discussing Tristan with her brother.

"Can you give me a better picture of how he attained his wealth? Please?" Giselle prodded Luc for more of what she likely didn't want to know.

Once she arrived in Montreal, she offered her nursing services anywhere she could help impoverished families. Her energy was limitless for them. There were so many underserved communities with families with upward of five children. When one got sick, they all did, and if the parents were ill as well, then food and survival also were issues. When the cold weather arrived, it would be even worse; it would be her childhood all over again.

Some of the families treated Giselle like a lifeline, and she saw the wanting for more in their eyes. They wanted her to make an ugly world good for them. They wanted her never to leave them—young, sick mothers exhausted from trying to care for too many babies, yet refusing to think there could be any other life. That was the frustrating part for Giselle.

In the evenings, with her daughters, she did her best to present a level, positive disposition. They still missed their father, and it was impossible for her to fill the void he had left. She felt it was best if she didn't even attempt to do so.

On several occasions Tristan had respectfully requested her company. As she had little free time now, they managed brief outings for dinner at one of his restaurants and occasionally dinner at his home. She, however, felt miles away from creating space for a new man in her life and also sensed his pain and guilt over the disappearance of Madeline. They were, by default and tragedy, kindred spirits. Eventually Tristan instigated a few subtle, exploratory conversations with her about meeting his mother. He felt they would like each other. Giselle, however, felt this could wait until the following summer.

She had made a few new acquaintances, but an odd feeling of deception always accompanied the process. She found it difficult to navigate small talk and get to know people while never being able to tell them she had taken a life, let alone disclose her tragedy of becoming a widow as a result of a random murder.

Tristan, however, never took her back to discussions of her previous life, nor she his, and it was understood they likely never would.

# CHAPTER 32
# MONTREAL

Luc's mind was somewhat more at ease now. The colder months were passing by, and his relationship with Tristan was strong. Even though Tristan kept his cards close to his chest, especially with matters regarding Giselle, Luc felt secure and stayed steadily on track with bringing in business.

He often thought of Mathew, and Tristan was expecting Luc to travel to the fellow's home community to check on his health.

"If you need to get back to see Mathew, things can be covered off here for as long as you need," Tristan benevolantly offered.

"We'll see. I want to be sure my sister is feeling strong." Luc's avoidance of a commital to check on

Mathew was noted by his boss but not questioned. There had been no explicit discussion between Luc and Tristan regarding the delays encountered at the start of the journey; Luc could see his sister was recovering emotionally and left well enough alone.

How different her life was now through Luc's eyes. The saintly, poverty-stricken shack of their childhood was far behind them, as was the small village with its decent lifestyle. Giselle also was spending a great deal of time in the company of Tristan in high style, in the heart of a city. She even had helped redecorate Aline's home with Tristan's mother, Siobhan, with whom she had formed an alliance. All this forward motion sat well with Luc, as well as Giselle. The rhythm of a new life held them tenderly, as if shielding them from their unbelievable past year.

Tristan received a terse message from the house staff that he was immediately required to meet with some of his men who operated only in Montreal. They were situated on the road at the front of his estate in two cars. Accompanied by two security men as usual, Tristan ventured out to see what the emergency was.

After he demanded an explanation from the quiet and strange group, a trusted employee, Sawyer Brash, spoke up.

"Sir, I have done some investigating and one of the new fellows heard some information you should know."

Sawyer was the epitomy of trustworthiness but Tristan was getting impatient and wanted to get to the heart of the issue. "I think I've worked out that it's definitely something I don't already know that I should so please continue."

Sawyer could be considered a bit on the simple side and frequently overrelated information. However, he had been along on many jobs and, while his communication skills were limited, his work ethic and dedication were not. He lowered his voice toward Tristan, as if the night wouldn't know their secrets. "The informant, sir, you know the one we pay that also works for the other side? He had a chance encounter on a train from Ottawa that the lads were on."

"Yes, and…?"

"It seems they were having a few drinks in the bar car with another gentleman, I think I have reason to believe you may have met him somewhere before. They were on about having something on you. Something you might want to pay out for. Pay out and edge out Mr. Boucher, sir."

Tristan was getting impatient and wanted to get to the essence of the issue. He glanced around and saw the informant in question. The informant kept his head down; he knew he could speak once the boss asked but until then kept quiet and led him to the second car where, restrained in the back, were his own Atlantic lads and a vaguely familiar face from Giselle's village: the mayor, Maxwell Loren. Rast and Sheen looked anxious to explain something and unhappy that they were being held against their wishes. The mayor demanded a conversation with Tristan with Rast and Sheen in attendance. Tristan instructed his men to escort them to a gazebo in the garden at the back of the property, where he would grant them a brief listen. His good humor was dissipating. Disappointment was setting in regarding the pair.

The security staff had called upon more of their own, unasked; they were efficient with predicting the possibility of an escalation of events. They were always ready with an assortment of tools, rope, and weapons.

The spring evening was cool and fresh, with an imminent rainfall in the air. Rast, Sheen, and Maxwell sat in the middle of the gazebo, with newly lit garden lamps and torches glowing around them. They couldn't see one another's faces, back to back, trussed up tightly.

Although he didn't show it, Tristan felt disappointment and disbelief. He had admired Rast and Sheen's spirit and was on his way to trusting them for bigger jobs. Hopefully the problem would turn out to be unfounded, but his gut feeling wasn't as such.

He sighed heavily. "All right, Rast, you go first. And I don't want any interruptions."

Rast's voice was raspy and shaky, and a cut over his right eye told Tristan he hadn't come along to explain himself agreeably. "Mr. Kaye, it's about Luc Boucher. When Stuart and I were preparing for the Lake Ontario trip, we came across something, by pure accident, sir. I think you'd be wise to inquire the lad himself."

*Inquire the lad?* Tristan was reminded of the pair's limited educational opportunities, and while their grammar was lacking, their conversational skills in general were not.

Rast continued. "On our trip to Loren, we saw Boucher and the other fellow from Muskrat Lake, the guide, dump a body in a marsh on the way to Jon Lewis's place. We was thinkin' it could be the missing son of that murderer who was bothering your intended lady. We also wondered if she had anything to do with it, as Lewis told Mr. Loren that he had overheard a conversation between the guide and Boucher telling it that way. The body had gunshots or stab wounds—lots of blood in any case."

Tristan stayed calm. "You were wondering if Giselle had something to do with this? Make sure that's what you intended to say or retract it immediately...And exactly why would you be concerned about a misstep with the law, given that's what we do for a living? Where, exactly, are you going with this tidbit of information, Rast?" Tristan had seen this kind of competitiveness and "ratting" before, even among men he'd thought were above it. Rast and Sheen were young and a bit too desperate, something he should have picked up on. He had bonded with them over shipyard knowledge—a mistake.

Rast was squirming now. "We was looking out for you, sir."

Tristan easily understood this part of it, but the real dilemma was why there was mention of a plot to extort money; he had to hear from them now. He turned to Sheen. "Do you have anything to add? I doubt it, but maybe this is your chance to not give Rast all the credit." Sheen said nothing.

The informant, as rough looking as any gangster, was given a terse nod to speak.

"I heard them, all right. I was on the last Sunday train from Ottawa. The three were talking about you, Mr. Kaye. They were cooking up a plan to press you for cash or they would initiate a meeting with police, regarding something you wouldn't like. Seeing that it involved your lady friend and Mr. Boucher, him being family practically, they figured you would pay and not bat an eye about letting him go. I think they would like to take his place. I guess that was before you got them tied up in your backyard, sir."

Tristan moved closer to all three; he was uncertain how to proceed, but they needed to learn his limits. He noticed the reeking scent of alcohol was high in the air. Had his men brought him drunks to deal with? They should know his stance on that by now. As he approached Maxwell Loren, who had been rather subdued so far, he observed his state. He was flushed and glassy eyed. Tristan asked him to explain his presence and relationship with Rast and Sheen.

Maxwell opened his mouth to speak and vomited copiously onto his legs, which didn't appear to faze him in the least. He coughed a little before letting Tristan know his thoughts. "I will not be tied up like a dog by an Irishman!" he bellowed. "This is not right!"

The mayor fell toward Rast, who cursed and looked at Sheen.

"We never should have let him at the booze," Sheen said, coming out of his silence. "He's nothing but an arse."

Tristan normally would have had his men dump them off a dock, but his curiosity was piqued by the insinuation of Giselle's knowledge of a dead body. He really just wanted to get back to his meal. There would be many questions from Giselle and Luc, so the matter had to be resolved at once. The informant would need to be compensated, even though Tristan was sure he worked for the West End Irish.

"I'm going to give you one opportunity to explain, Mr. Loren, as best you can, why you're with Rast and Sheen." Tristan was still calm; Rast and Sheen were dying to speak more but knew better.

"You don't know who I am, do you?" Maxwell slurred. "I'm highly respected and connected, and you would do well to let me go! These two sots are nothing to me. They gave me some information and led me here. I paid them well."

"Why?" Tristan moved even closer, despite the smell.

"To take you down a notch or two, sir. You should know how this works..." He was getting sick again. "These two are amateurs, but I'm a businessman with much to offer." He wasn't making sense.

Rast and Sheen were shaking their heads and cursing. Maxwell continued his drunken rant but was choking, coughing, and coming to tears. "We could have had a damn good marriage. I don't know how she put up with that bore of a blacksmith. The problem was that you showed up, taking advantage of a vulnerable widow. That would have required an incredible amount of intelligence and wit, wouldn't it?"

That statement held all the information Tristan needed regarding what to do with this idiot. Maxwell Loren had designs on Giselle and had used the Atlantic lads to find Tristan. But he would need to keep the good mayor alive and upright until he found out what—other than his being scorned—had brought him to Montreal. At least he could connect how the lads and Loren, in the spirit of attaining something each longed for, hoped Luc and Giselle would fall from his favor. But he needed more details.

Rast interrupted his thoughts. "You do know something funny went on at the beginning of the Lake Ontario trip, sir. We had an unnecessary delay because of Boucher and the guide, and I doubt any of it was explained to you. Me and Sheen think it has to do with your lady friend and the body."

Maxwell was like a caged animal now; the confinement was stressing him, and his rage surfaced. "Shut up, both of you!" He looked up at Tristan. "I don't care about the damn body or that these two idiots might want you to pay them off—I have more intelligence than all of you put together. I arranged for that bloody blacksmith to die, and I'll have all of you at the gates of hell by tomorrow! Let me go!" He was sweating, his eyes bulging in his stupor.

"You might want to explain that in detail." Tristan turned to one of the house staff and quietly ordered him to get Luc.

Tristan produced a small handgun from his coat pocket and pointed it at the mayor. He waited until Luc appeared and motioned for him to keep quiet. "I want to hear how Giselle's husband died by your arrangements," he told Maxwell.

Luc's full attention was turned on Maxwell, even more so than Tristan's was.

The mayor scoffed. "That goddamned German and his family were starving. His vile temper made him an easy target. I told him that idiot Reicher hated farmers and wanted to eliminate them all. I told him I would pay him royally to rough him up or finish him. It was easy—bloody village idiot."

Luc, white faced, was quickly restrained by three men. Tristan was saddened that Luc had received this news about his brother-in-law and felt sickened that Giselle soon would discover her husband's murder wasn't just a random mad act but the calculated plot of a third person. Still, he wanted to know about the "delay" Rast had mentioned—and of course about the body.

Luc gathered himself and began the story for his boss. "My sister is a decent woman who didn't deserve any of this horseshit, beginning with Josef's death, you know? She's strong—too strong for her own good—and she took care of the situation with the farmer's son. While Mathew and I were taking care of business, young Ivan decided to retaliate and send her and the mayor, I think, to meet their maker. He blamed them for his father's suicide."

Luc slowed down his speech, lowered his voice, and faced Tristan directly. "Ivan was creeping around the house one night, making threats, and she shot him."

"Shot him?" Tristan exhaled.

"I had shown her how to use my shotgun. Mathew and I disposed of the body at the outset of the trip, on our way to Jon Lewis's place. Only I had no idea how spiritual Mathew is. Once he discovered the farmer and his son were 'bad spirits,' as he said, he needed us to purify our own spirits and set us on a journey of isolation in the bush. If we survived, we'd know we never would be touched by the spirits of Hauffe and his son. It set us back, but we made it, didn't we? That's all."

"That's all?" Tristan repeated sarcastically, shaking his head. "I think I should have been informed. Why wouldn't Giselle have told me what she had done?"

Tristan, then quickly realizing he wasn't in a setting for a discussion regarding an issue between Giselle and himself, quietly and privately instructed his men to take the three to the docks, where they would be shot and their bodies disposed of in the St.

Lawrence River. After pondering the situation for a moment, he gave his men new orders and then headed into the house with Luc.

They found Giselle at a window in the living room; she had asked to be left alone until the pair returned to the house. It was several hours past dinner, and no one was interested in food. Tristan faced Giselle. "Why didn't you confide in me?"

The answer didn't come from Giselle even though she took a breath to speak.

"I would have done the same thing. I would have kept it inside. You don't have to explain to me."

He was getting good at recognizing their similarities, comparing their behavior and decisions.

She was stoic. "The thought of the extent of Maxwell Loren's obsession with me is vile—the worst part is how I didn't pick up on it."

Although they had lived in the same village for years, she never had detected any apparent manifestation of his feelings for her. She smoothed her dress and pulled her shawl more tightly around her. It was unthinkable that Maxwell's feelings went so far as for him to arrange her husband's death to make her available to him. Did he really think he could mold the universe? He was in a delusional state for certain.

Tristan ventured to say dryly, "This will be a lovely story about you to share with my mother at next Sunday's dinner."

# CHAPTER 33
# EMBARKING

B lindfolded and stumbling, Rast, Sheen, and
Maxwell were shoved along the shipyard walkway
by several members of Tristan's staff. The mayor was
showing signs of illness—self-induced but nonetheless foul. As they were lacking one of their primary
senses, their hearing and sense of smell were heightened. The air was salty but only from the older vessels docked there that had soaked in the seawater for
years. The great river was fresh.

An unsettling quietness revealed they were walking in a less-traveled area, which made the three uneasy. Rast and Sheen were shaking with uncertainty;
when they asked any questions or spoke to one another, one of Tristan's men jabbed them with a billy club.

The three were halted by their captors and then unexpectedly shoved forward down a ramp. The distinct sensation of navigating a gangway was detectable to the two younger men, but it had been a while since Maxwell had boarded a vessel.

"Keep moving!" one of Tristan's men demanded.

They stumbled down into a hull that didn't smell all that unpleasant. A faint sweetness wafted amid the typical mustiness.

After a firm closing of the hatch, they heard an indistinct conversation between an unfamiliar voice and their captors. Several hours later two armed sailors appeared, removed their blindfolds, smiled at them, and disappeared back to the deck.

They couldn't manage to pick the lock but were left scraps, water, and buckets. No matter how much they yelled, their calls went unanswered. They did quiet after the night gently pulled their sense of balance away from them; the vessel was sailing.

One week later Tristan and Giselle left morning Mass at St. Louis de France Church. Their presence there as a couple was a bold statement, but as she and her daughters were now residents of Montreal, she felt more than entitled to attend church with whomever she pleased. They both lingered to greet and talk with acquaintances on the steps and street before getting into the waiting car.

They were headed to Aline's; the girls had opted to sleep in and knew their mother would always let church be a choice. She could almost hear Father Gaston's protests: "The young people should be made to attend, plain and simple. As a mother you should be a benevolent dictator."

She wondered about him and for a moment longed to be back in her village with Josef and her old life. There were no choices about some things, however, including the deaths of loved ones and also getting on with life and making changes.

Whenever the looming darkness from the past year crept into her thoughts, she quickly shifted her focus to her daughters and to Tristan's dependable strength and kindness. She could live with what had transpired, which was made possible by deciding not to judge herself or others. Could she really perceive herself to be different from the desperate man who had altered her family's lives forever?

"Don't worry, love," Tristan had told her. "He's en route to Halifax and then the Caribbean with the other two."

Tristan sensed her thoughts drifting and offered a somewhat startling, yet not entirely unsuspected, suggestion for travel for all of them. "We should visit my home in Ireland and my brother. I have nephews the same age as your daughters." Giselle looked stricken. He continued, saying, "A long overseas vacation is usually welcomed by those who lead lives like ours." He was joking, but she knew he also was letting her know that there was no going back to innocence once one had departed from it abruptly, as she had. He knew that firsthand.

"How long does it take to cross? More specifically, how long shall we stay?" Giselle wasn't certain about it, as the VON and other interests were keeping her grounded. A lengthy absence didn't tempt her as it did him.

In a steady, hopeful voice, Tristan told her, "My family is, as we speak, building a premium ocean liner. It will be luxurious and most comfortable. If we go this time next year, we can sail home from Ireland to New York, first class, on a maiden voyage."

Made in the USA
Charleston, SC
26 October 2015